The Wonder Kid

The Wonder Kid

www.houghtonmifflinbooks.com

The text of this book is set in Sabon.
Book design by Joyce White

Library of Congress Cataloging-in-Publication Data

Harrar, George, 1949-
  The wonder kid / by George Harrar ; [illustrated by] Anthony Winiarski.
      p. cm.
  "A portion of this novel first appeared in the <u>Dickinson Review</u>, 1999."
  Summary: In the summer of 1954, eleven-year-old Jesse James MacLean contracts polio, but with a friend's help and despite his unsympathetic father, he finds ways to prove that his spirit is still strong.
  ISBN 0-618-56317-2 (hardcover)
  [1. Poliomyelitis—Fiction. 2. Fathers and sons—Fiction. 3. Friendship—Fiction.]
I. Winiarski, Anthony, ill. II. Title.
  PZ7.H2346Won 2006
  [Fic]—dc22
2005019080

ISBN-13: 978-0618-56317-3

Manufactured in the United States of America
QUM 10 9 8 7 6 5 4 3 2 1

The Wonder Kid

George Harrar

Illustrations by
Anthony Winiarski

Houghton Mifflin Company
Boston 2006

To Myles, Andrew, Jordan, David, Paige,
Gabrielle, Kyle, Emily, Kelly, Katharine, and Charlotte,
who are growing up without the fear of polio.

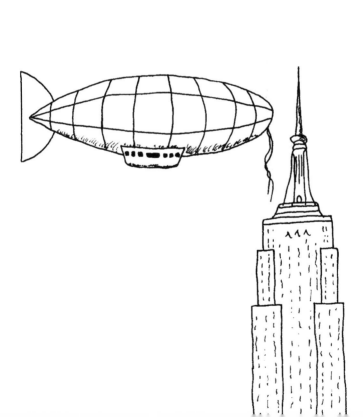

Chapter 1
YOU WON'T BELIEVE THIS

I remember being born.

Nobody believes me when I tell them that, but I do. What I remember is a sharp jab in my stomach that hurt so bad I wondered, *What kind of world is this where they make you cry as soon as you get here?*

Okay, newborn babies don't think, right? But how do you know that? Just because they can't tell you they're thinking doesn't mean they aren't.

I'll prove I remember being born. My grandfather came to live with us when I was eleven because he had a tricky heart and needed help taking care of himself. He moved into the spare room next to mine on the second floor. I told Gramps one day that all my friends were born in hospitals but I was born right in our living room. He said, "You don't have to tell me, Jesse. I was the one who delivered you."

That was news to me, and I had all sorts of questions about the night I "popped into the world," as he put it. He remembered it being uncommonly rainy for August. He was staying overnight with my mom because Dad wasn't home from the war yet—I'll tell you more about that later. Gramps made spaghetti for dinner, with his special meatballs, which were as big as baseballs. They had just finished cleaning up the dishes when Mom slumped into a chair and said, "The baby's coming."

Gramps figured it was the meatballs talking, since he had made them extra spicy.

Then she yelled, "The baby's coming *right now,*" which surprised him, because she didn't normally raise her voice. "There's no time to go to the hospital."

That was fine with Gramps. He said women had been having babies at home for as long as there had been women and didn't need doctors getting in the way. So he got my mother onto the sofa and found towels and water and then held her hand as she pushed me out of her.

"Your head came fast," he said, "but then it was like you couldn't decide whether you wanted to be born or not. I had to grab hold of your ears and pull."

I told Gramps that I remembered being jabbed in the stomach, and he said, "That was me. My hand slipped when I was cutting the cord to your mother, and the scissors poked your middle. I thought I'd killed you by how hard you cried."

So there's my proof—I remember being born!

Chapter 2
PLAYING WAR ALONE

Summer is when you're supposed to have all sorts of fun, like one long recess. No writing reports on dead presidents. No making maps of South America where you paste cotton and coffee beans on different countries. No sitting at a desk for six hours keeping your head down so the teacher won't call on you. Best of all, no getting up at six a.m.

Well, 1954, when Gramps moved in with us, started out as the Summer of No Fun—and it was all because of polio. Getting overheated was a sure-fire way of catching "President Roosevelt's disease," as my mother called it, so I wasn't allowed to go to the playground or pretty much anywhere else. It was a boring time to be a kid.

President Roosevelt wasn't president anymore, since he had died in 1945. I did a report on him for my social studies class. He caught polio when he was already grown up, which was unusual, since it usually struck kids. He couldn't walk without somebody holding his arm to make sure he didn't fall over. But people still elected him president four times, which is more than anybody else. Mom says most folks didn't even know he had the disease, because they never saw him in his wheelchair.

Anyway, polio was back again the summer of '54. For some reason it always appeared along with the heat. It scared people even more than Martians landing in a spaceship because at least you could *see* them. Polio was invisible until it hit you, and then it was like catching a terrible flu that you couldn't get rid of.

Kids got it the worst. Sometimes polio attacked the muscles that controlled their legs and made them paralyzed. Other times polio struck their lungs and they couldn't breathe right. These kids ended up inside iron lungs, which were huge machines that pumped air in and out of them. The iron lung was about the scariest thing that could happen to a kid. Only your head stuck out. Sometimes you had to stay in there for years.

The luckier kids only needed braces on their

legs to help them walk again. Those were the ones you saw on the March of Dimes posters. That was the charity President Roosevelt started to raise money to help polio kids. After I finished my report on him, I sent in five dimes.

No one knew for sure how you caught the disease, which made everybody nervous. Mom wouldn't let me play with my friends for fear polio was hiding somewhere in their bodies, waiting to infect me. Summer playground was canceled, and my Cub Scout troop disbanded because just one boy, Ricky, showed up. Ricky's parents let him do anything, which is probably why he had three broken bones and two concussions and one snake bite just in the first year I knew him.

Luckily I had my dog, Gort, to play with. He's the mutt I picked out at the animal shelter on my ninth birthday. Sometimes you look at him and think he's a spaniel, other times he looks like a beagle or collie. Dad wanted me to choose a puppy, but when I poked my finger through Gort's cage, he licked it, and I knew he was for me. He was six at the time—about forty in human years, which is awfully old—but I didn't care. He was a stray who needed a home. They were going to put him to sleep if somebody didn't take him. I named him Gort because I'd just seen the movie *The Day the Earth Stood Still*. Gort's the robot from outer space who would do anything to save his master, Klaatu, including destroying the world, unless Klaatu said the special words "Klaatu *barada nikto.*" That meant something like "Klaatu says, don't kill everything!"

My dog and I had an awful lot of time that summer and not much to do. I pulled out my chemistry set and made ink and a pad to take everybody's fingerprints. I even took Gort's pawprint, which was a mistake because he ran out before I could wipe off the ink and he got it on the hall carpet.

I imagined a murder had happened right in our house, and I was the detective tracking down the killer. It was like in Clue, except we didn't have any Library or Ballroom or Lounge for the scene of the crime. I don't think we had a Conservatory either, but I'm not sure what one of those is. Gort was my trusty companion, ready to bite any bad guys who threatened me—unless I said the special words, of course.

The other thing I did a lot that summer was

draw. I was pretty good at copying things I could see, such as a hand, like this one:

It's kind of gory, I know, with the nail through it. I drew this after reading a comic called the *Crypt of Terror*. I wanted to draw a person to go with the hand, but I'm terrible at doing bodies. They look like they're made of sticks.

Mom only let me go outside in the cooler parts of the day, such as early morning or late afternoon. Even then Gort and I had to stay in our backyard, which was exactly sixty Jesse-steps long and forty-seven Jesse-steps wide. I built myself a high jump by stacking two columns of old bricks as the supports and balancing a thin branch between them. The highest I ever jumped over was two feet, two inches. I don't know whether that's good or not. Probably not, because I'm not really an athlete. Gort jumped even higher than me, but that's because I held his favorite biscuit over the stick.

When I got tired of jumping, I lay back in the grass and stared up into the sky, wondering what was up there. Sometimes I saw a jet leaving a long white trail of exhaust. It amazed me to think that a man could be sitting inside a plane that seemed so small. I probably seemed small to him, too.

Every afternoon I played war under our giant copper beech tree. I arranged my army men among the roots that stuck up from the ground like giant knuckles. When Mom took her nap, I made paper airplanes and then lit them on fire to dive-bomb the cardboard forts on the ground. I imagined the garden hose as a giant cannon and doused the enemy army with jets of water.

Mom didn't like me playing war all the time. She said she wished somebody would figure out a way for boys to *play peace*. We both thought for a bit on that, but neither of us could think of a fun way to do it.

Chapter 3
SKINLESS FRANK

My father hated unexplained noises, and our old Buick Special had a million of them. Early that summer he packed us into the car and drove us upstate for the motorcycle races. He called it a family outing even though Gramps and Gort stayed with neighbors, Mom kept her hands over her ears most of the time, and I ended up coughing from the dust kicked up on the track. She wanted to get me checked for asthma, but Dad said that was a waste of money. He knew what was wrong: my lungs were puny, just like the rest of me. He told her that when he didn't know I was listening.

I wanted to enjoy the races. It was exciting to see the cycles zooming around the curves, banking so far inside it looked like they might fall over. I could never tell who was ahead, so I just cheered whenever Dad did. A couple of times he slapped me on the back and said, "Look at that!"

I had never heard anything as loud as fifty engines roaring at the same time. The sound was like thousands of giant bees swarming around your head. After the race was over I could still hear those engines in my ears for hours.

Dad looked for shortcuts on the way home, and we ended up taking roads that weren't even on the map. I liked staying on the main highway to see the billboards for Burma-Shave, which is a shaving cream. There were usually six billboards, one after another. Mom and I read them together out loud. This was our favorite, which we repeated to each other for miles:

HE LIT A MATCH

TO CHECK GAS TANK

THAT'S WHY

THEY CALL HIM

SKINLESS FRANK

BURMA-SHAVE

I imagined Skinless Frank walking around with his insides outside, like this:

I pictured him eating a hot dog at the amusement park. It would tumble down his throat into his stomach, be mashed up there, and then be shot out the other end of him. It was a pretty disgusting image to have in your head.

Then I thought it might be so disgusting that it would make a great horror movie—*The Invasion of the Skinless Men!* There could be a whole horde of skinless zombies taking over the earth. Mom said she wasn't sure people would sit in a theater for two hours looking at skinless men. I said that kids would, at least the boys, and maybe even a few girls I knew.

Anyway, we were barreling down one bumpy old back road when Dad raised his hand, the signal for us to be quiet. He cocked his head, trying to adjust his ears to the noise he heard.

"In the trunk," he said after a minute. He pulled off the road by a cornfield, and I got out with him to check. We looked for anything loose, like the spare tire. He ran his hand over the wires to the rear lights. Everything seemed tight. I felt like I was helping.

"Get in," he said, and I started back to my seat. "No, get in *here*." His long, thick finger pointed inside the trunk. Could he really mean that? I couldn't even stand the sheets tucked in too tight around me in bed at night. When our class trip went to Lost River Caverns, only me and one other kid were allowed to stay above ground. I was claustrophobic, like Gramps. Didn't Dad know that about me?

"Get in there now," he said a second time, and I knew he wouldn't say it again. I could see Mom's eyes in the rearview mirror as she pretended to fix her hair. I wanted to call to her, but what could she do? She had never crossed him in my whole life. My only chance was to run into the field and lose myself in the cornstalks forever. Running away often seemed like a good idea in my family, but I could never figure out where to run to.

"I know plenty of eleven-year-olds who would

do this," Dad said, and I thought, *Then why don't you get yourself one of those kids and leave me alone!* Before I could run he grabbed me by my belt and stuffed me into the trunk. With a flick of his hand he shut the lid. I felt buried inside the world, with everyone else on the outside.

"It's time you faced your fears," I heard him say in his gruff voice, the one he used with me a lot. It sounded like he was speaking to me through a pillow. "Stop whimpering," he said, "and listen for the rattle."

We bounced down the road for what seemed like miles, my head banging, my ears flooded with all sorts of sounds. I twisted around and pushed against the backseat with my feet, hoping that I could force it down. I kicked and kicked, but nothing happened. I was trapped. My mind reeled with the possibilities, and they were all bad. What if he got into an accident? Nobody would know I was in here. What if . . .

The car stopped. I counted one, two, three . . . to ten. It couldn't take more than ten seconds for him to get out and open the trunk. What was he doing?

The car started again, rolling me against the

back. Was he going to drive all the way home like this? There wasn't enough air. I'd suffocate.

"Mom," I yelled because I figured it was no use calling to him, "Mom, get me out, PLEASE!"

The car stopped again. I counted again, and by the time I reached ten, the trunk opened. Climbing out, I blinked in the bright sun.

Dad stood in front of me, his hands folded across his chest. "Well, where's the noise coming from?"

When I couldn't tell him, he spit on the ground at my feet and shook his head.

I got back into the car and Mom patted my arm. "I'm sorry, Jesse," she said, "I'm really sorry."

Chapter 4
THE UGLY SCAR THAT I HAD TO SEE

I was what they called a war baby, born in August 1942. The Japanese attacked Pearl Harbor eight months before, which is when we joined World War II, and we dropped the A-bomb on Hiroshima exactly three years after my birth date, the sixth. They called that A-bomb Little Boy, which seems like a strange name for something that killed a whole city full of people. Why not Mega Blast or The Destroyer? At least it should have been called Big Boy.

Not many kids were born in those war years because millions of men were off in Europe fighting the Germans or in the South Pacific fighting the Japanese. My dad fought, too, as a gunner on the aircraft carrier *Yorktown*. He helped stop the Japs from taking over the little island of Midway, which is on the other side of the world in the Pacific Ocean. During this battle the

Japanese planes dropped bombs on the *Yorktown*, and an enemy pilot did a kamikaze dive right into the control tower. The explosion sent shrapnel flying everywhere, Dad said. One piece blew into his right arm just as the *Yorktown* started to sink. He jumped into the water to save himself.

The doctors decided they'd have to cut out too much of his arm to get to the shrapnel, so they left it in. The guys at school didn't believe it when I told them my dad had a piece of metal in his arm. They wanted to know what it looked like. I couldn't tell them because he wouldn't show me. He always wore long sleeves, even in summer. Sometimes I tried to sneak a peek at his arm when he was dressing in the morning, but I never got close enough to see anything. Once when he was shaving I walked into the bathroom as if by mistake, but he yelled at me so loud I shut the door fast.

I had to see his scar. It was like an obsession, something I couldn't get out of my head. So on my last birthday, when I blew out the candles on my cake, Mom told me to make a wish and I said, "I wish to see the shrapnel in Dad's arm."

"You just wasted a perfectly good wish," Dad

said as he sliced my special banana cake.

"I bet you don't even have a scar," I said, like I had planned. "I bet you just made it all up." I figured he might roll up his sleeve just to prove me wrong. He liked to prove me wrong.

"Don't bet too much," he said as he stuck a big forkful of my cake in his mouth. "You'd lose."

"Oh, Jack," Mom said, "let him look once and then maybe he'll stop thinking about it."

"Is that right, boy? You see it once, then you'll stop bugging me about it?"

"Sure, Dad, anything you say."

He stuck another piece in his mouth. "Maybe after I'm done. This is awful good birthday cake."

It seemed to me he was chewing each bite extra long. Why do you even have to chew cake? You just put it in your mouth, swish the icing around on your tongue, then swallow. But Dad kept chewing and chewing. When he finished his piece, which was about twice as big as the one he gave me, he cut himself another.

"Stop teasing him, Jack," Mom said.

"Okay, take your look." He pushed up his sleeve. There, just above his elbow, was a scar twice the size of my longest finger. I couldn't stop staring at it. "Go on," he said, "you might as well touch it, too."

I ran my finger up and down the scar. It was very smooth because there was no hair growing on it. Beneath the scar I saw an odd dark patch. That had to be the shrapnel. I poked there a few times but couldn't feel the metal underneath.

"Doesn't your arm hurt with the shrapnel in there, Dad?"

"Only when I use it," he said with a laugh. I guess that meant it always hurt, because a person uses his arms to do just about everything.

Dad dropped his sleeve and reached for more cake. Suddenly the scar was gone. I might never see it again. I closed my eyes and pictured it in my head so that I'd remember it forever.

"I wish I had a scar like that," I said.

Mom grabbed my arm. "Jesse! Such a terrible thing to wish for."

The war injury kept Dad from being a carpenter, which is what he always wanted to be since he was my age. He couldn't lift things for very long or hammer for very long or do pretty much anything with his right arm for very long. I knew it hurt bad, even though he never said so. Lots of times when he was doing work around the house he'd grunt and rub the area around the scar. When we played catch outside, he couldn't even throw the ball to me overhand. That was okay, though, because his underhand was plenty hard enough for me.

The navy decided they couldn't use Dad with his bad arm, so they shipped him home in October. He didn't miss much of my life—I was still only two months old.

It took me a while to figure out how that baby-making stuff works. It didn't seem like anybody was going to tell me, so I looked it up in books at the library. I didn't dare bring them home where Mom or Dad might see them. They would think I was weird or something. I wasn't even sure the librarian would let a kid check out a book on making babies. So I learned what I needed from standing in the back aisle reading *The Facts of Life*. I held it inside another book so anybody walking by couldn't tell what I was reading.

One fact of life I learned is that a baby gets half its genes from its mother and half from its father. If that's so, where were my father's genes in me? I have brown hair like my mother and brown eyes like my mother and light skin like my mother and long eyelashes like my mother and small feet like my mother. I even sneeze like my mother—two quick gasps and then *KA-CHOO!* so loud it could wake up the dead.

Dad told me once that I looked more like the milkman than him. I think that was a joke, but he didn't laugh when he said it. For days after that I tried to wake up extra early to see the delivery man from Taylor's Dairy leaving the quart bottle of milk on our porch. But I always fell back to sleep before he got there, so I never got to see whether I looked like him or not.

Chapter 5
"HEY, SKINNY!"

You ever see an ad in a magazine and think, *This is talking to me?*

It happened when Mom took me to Dr. Metz for my annual physical. I thought that since I was eleven she wouldn't go into the exam room, but when I started down the hall, she followed me. I said, "You can wait out there, Mom."

"Don't be silly," she said. "I always come in with you."

So I went in and began undressing like Dr. Metz asked with my mother sitting there telling him how many rashes and cysts and warts I'd gotten this year. She was making me sound like a leper. Besides, he already knew all this. She dragged me in there every time something strange popped up on my body. He was the one who rubbed salve on my rashes and burned the warts off my hands with dry ice.

I unbuttoned my shirt and bent over to pull off my loafers and socks.

"Hurry up, Jesse," Mom said. "The doctor doesn't have all day."

There was only one thing left to go—my pants. I unhooked my belt and started to unzip, but my hand froze.

"What is it?" she said. "The zipper stuck?"

"Yeah, that's it, the zipper's stuck."

"Here, let me try."

This was terrible—Mom unzipping me!

"No, that's okay," I said fast. "I'll get it."

"You know, Mrs. MacLean," the doctor said, "I think there's some paperwork you need to take care of with my nurse. Why don't you do that while I examine Jesse?"

"That's a good idea, Mom."

She stood up. "Well, if you don't mind being by yourself."

Mind? Was she crazy?

"I really don't mind, Mom."

After she left, Dr. Metz said, "Let's see about that zipper."

"Oh, it's okay now," I said, "see?" I slipped out of my pants and stood there in my white Fruit of the Looms. I didn't like anybody seeing me in my underpants, but at least it wasn't Mom.

Dr. Metz did all his usual checks on me, such as listening to my heart and lungs, and looking down my throat and in my ears. When you think of all the places a doctor has to look into on people, it's a wonder anyone wants to be one. They must make an awful lot of money.

He got me on the scale and lowered the metal bar on my head. "Four feet eight," he said. "That's within the normal range for your age." Then he checked my weight—eighty-four pounds. "A bit on the skinny side," he said.

I looked sideways at the mirror on the wall and saw my whole, almost naked self. That was a shock. At home there was only the little mirror over the bathroom sink that showed the upper half of me. The doctor was right: I was as skinny as a beanpole.

For the next ten minutes he listened to my heart and lungs and other things inside me. Then he said, "You can get dressed now, Jesse."

As I pulled on my pants, I saw the top of a *Reader's Digest* magazine in the wall rack. The headline said, "Hey, Skinny, Yer Ribs Are Showing."

I looked back in the mirror. My ribs *were* showing. How did the magazine know that?

"I'll call your mother in," Dr. Metz said, and I hurried to put my shirt on. Then I grabbed the magazine. There was a picture of the strongest man I had ever seen.

He had more muscles than Dad. He had muscles on top of muscles. He had muscles where I didn't even know you could have them. Under the picture it said: "Charles Atlas, who holds the title of the world's most perfectly developed man." In larger print the ad said: "I Can Make *YOU* A New Man, Too, In Only 15 Minutes A Day!"

I didn't need to become a new man, but I did like the idea of having muscles as big as those of Charles Atlas. Then I wouldn't be puny anymore. Nobody would make fun of me, even Dad.

Dr. Metz said I could take the magazine home, since it was an old issue. The next day I cut out the coupon from the ad, which promised to send me a thirty-two-page booklet absolutely FREE, "crammed with photographs, answers to vital questions, and valuable advice." There was even a box for me to check if I was under fourteen, which I was, so that they would send me Booklet A. Booklet A, I guessed, was for skinny kids like me.

I addressed an envelope to Mr. Charles Atlas in New York, stuck on a three-cent stamp, and sent the coupon on its way. I felt sure that my life was about to change.

Chapter 6
GRAMPS GOES BANANAS

My grandfather moved in with us right before school let out in June. Dad wasn't happy about it, but Mom said it was her father, and family had to help out family.

Dad and Gramps never got along. "We don't see eye to eye" was all Gramps would say about it. Dad wouldn't say anything at all.

Gramps was so weak some days that he had to stay in bed. It was my job to run things up to him. He said it was only fitting—he helped me into the world, I should help him out of it. I didn't like when he talked about dying. I wanted him to live with us forever, because he was fun to be around. Plus, whenever Dad was on the warpath, I could always escape by saying I had something to do for Gramps.

Each morning I carried up his breakfast tray loaded with toast, black coffee, grapefruit juice, and the *Philadelphia Inquirer* newspaper. Sometimes Mom added an apple or banana. Gramps would lift it to his eye and inspect it like a diamond. If he saw a mark he'd start ranting about bad fruit. Once he squashed a banana under his fist and another time he tossed an apple under the chair. It was pretty funny. I always hoped he'd find a bruise.

One day I asked him why fruit got him so upset. "I grew up on a farm," he said, "and my father always sent the good crops to market and fed us the seconds. That wasn't fair. I helped grow the fruit, so I should have had some of the sweet apples instead of the falls."

"What're the falls?" I asked.

"They're the apples that fall from the tree before you can pick them. They get all bruised and wormy lying on the ground. Those are the ones we had to eat, and I'm not doing it anymore. That's a prerogative of living so long."

"What's a pa-rogative?"

"It's *prerogative*, and it means your right to do something or not do something."

Nobody ever told me I had any prerogative. In fact, I don't remember my mother or father ever saying I had the right to do or not to do any single thing. Seemed like I never had a choice at all.

Eating peas, for example. There was a food I wouldn't have minded tossing on the floor. One time I was playing with the little green peas that come in Swanson's Turkey and Stuffing TV dinner, trying to balance as many as I could on my knife. I'd gotten to five. Sometimes if I stalled long enough Dad would go out back to smoke a Camel and Mom would start clearing dishes and I could sneak the peas into my pocket or some other place she wouldn't look. One time she stayed there watching me, and then she started singing:

> *I eat my peas with honey,*
> *I've done it all my life.*
> *It makes the peas taste funny,*
> *But it keeps them on my knife.*

I said maybe I'd like peas better with honey on them, but she said it wasn't right to smother good vegetables in sugar. So I ended up sliding the peas into my mouth with the knife and swallowing them without them ever touching my tongue. Mom said, "How can you know you don't like peas if you never chew them?" That was easy to answer—some things you know taste bad just by looking at them. Besides, she'd used that argument to get me to try Brussels sprouts, and I gagged on them.

What it came down to was that I had to eat whatever was set before me at dinner, even if it included peas and Brussels sprouts, sometimes on the same plate! It isn't fair that adults can use a word like "prerogative" in order to do what they want and not do what they don't want. Words should be for everyone.

At first I spilled Gramps's coffee no matter how carefully I carried it up the steps to his room. He told me to stop staring at the tray and let my hands take care of the balance without my eyes interfering. I tried that and sure enough, it worked. By not thinking of doing something, I could do it perfectly.

When I got to his room I never had any hands free to knock, so I banged my head on the door. He'd always growl, "Who's that bothering me at this ungodly hour?" I'd push the door in with my foot, and

Gramps would be sitting up in bed, his napkin already stuck under his chin. I knew he was hungry and ready to eat, but he pretended I was waking him. He'd rub his eyes and shake his head. "Can't an old man sleep through the morning if he wants to? What have I got to get up for?"

I'd make up something important—"The pipes burst overnight, Grandpa, and the water is filling up the first floor already, so you better eat fast." Or, "We're moving to Timbuktu today and you're coming with us, so Mom says to hurry up and pack."

"All in good time," he'd say. "That's the secret of growing old, take everything in good time."

Chapter 7
LANDING ON THE EMPIRE STATE BUILDING

My father had the habit of taking off for days or even a week at a time, and he seemed to do it even more that summer of '54. Maybe he was trying to get away from Gramps. Dad seemed upset just having him upstairs in the guest room.

I never knew where exactly my father went on his trips or when he'd turn up again. He'd say to Mom, "I'm starting up a new territory this week, so I may be gone for a while," and she'd nod and kiss him goodbye. I never heard her ask him any questions, so I figured I shouldn't ask, either. We both acted like this was the normal way a family worked. Gramps said that Dad was one of those men who needed to be on the road. He told me not to worry.

Sometimes when I was out buying groceries with

Mom, people would say to her that they'd seen Dad in the next county and ask what he was doing over there. She always said he was on business. Since Dad was a Fuller Brush man, that sort of made sense, but it was hard to understand why he'd be away for so long at a time. He was only selling brushes, after all, like hairbrushes and scrub brushes and even horse brushes. He'd knock on people's doors and show them his samples, hoping they'd order. It's not as though he was a banker, like Joey's dad, who took the airplane to Chicago and the train to New York sometimes.

I'd never been farther away than Philadelphia to see the Liberty Bell, and that's only twelve miles from this little place called Jenkintown where I lived. Philadelphia was okay, but what I wanted to set my eyes on was New York. I had a booklet on it called *New York, The Wonder City*. It said that the Empire State Building was the world's tallest building—one hundred and two floors. It took more than a minute to ride to the top in an elevator. I'd never been in one of those. I sure wanted to in order to see the mooring they put on top so that blimps could land there and drop off their passengers. I imagined how it would look:

Dad said that was a lamebrained idea, because nobody in their right mind would climb out of a blimp a quarter mile into the sky. He said aircraft should be kept away from buildings that tall to avoid flying into them, which actually happened in 1945. Luckily the Empire State Building didn't fall over from being hit by the plane, but fourteen people died. Dad could remember the details of all kinds of disasters, like the *Titanic* sinking and the *Hindenburg* blimp crashing. He was pretty interesting that way.

My booklet said that Manhattan, which is the central part of New York City, used to belong to the Indians. A Dutch man named Peter Minuit paid them $24 worth of trinkets for the whole island. I don't know exactly what trinkets are, but they couldn't be very valuable if they were worth only $24. I had $27.82 saved up in the bank, which meant that me, a regular old almost-twelve-year-old, could have bought the whole city. Of course, like Mom says, $24 went a lot further back in the 1600s when the Indians lived in Manhattan.

I read more than ever that summer. By July 1 I'd already gone through four Hardy Boys books: *The*

Yellow Feather Mystery, *The Secret of the Caves*, *The Sinister Sign Post*, and *Footprints Under the Window*. I liked reading all about Frank and Joe's adventures, but I really wished I could have some of my own. I kept an eye out for a yellow feather or secret cave or sinister signpost. All Gort and I ever found were a few footprints under the dining room window, which turned out to be from Dad putting in the screens.

I also read sports books like *Hoop Crazy* and *A Pass and a Prayer*. I knew I'd never grow up to be a star like Chip Hilton. But when I read about him making the winning shot or throwing the winning pass, I felt like a star, at least until I closed the book. Then I was back to being Jesse James MacLean, a shrimpy sort of kid who threw a baseball like a girl. Actually, in gym some of the girls threw the ball *better* than I did. That was embarrassing.

Chapter 8
CHICKEN LEGS

With Dad gone so often and Mom working part-time selling shoes at Goldberg's uptown, I spent most of my day with Gramps. You could say I was babysitting him, except he wasn't a baby and I didn't get paid.

One Saturday when I went up to his room, he was in a bad mood. "Open those curtains," he ordered me, and I pulled back the white curtains across the front windows. Mom had just washed and ironed them, so they smelled fresh. "You see any rain?" he said.

I shook my head. "There's some clouds, but no rain, Gramps."

He picked up his transistor radio and shook it. "Then why are these fools canceling a double-header?"

"Must be raining in the city."

"We're almost in the city ourselves. How can it be so all-fired rainy there and just a little cloudy here?"

I shrugged because I didn't know. Besides, there was no reasoning with Gramps when his Phillies game was rained out. The only thing worse was when it wasn't raining and his Phillies were losing, which was happening a lot lately. Then you didn't even want to stick your head in his room for fear he would chew it off.

Gramps set the radio on his night table, and I spotted a plastic bag of sourballs sitting there. He saw me and held out the bag. "Take one."

I did, and then he did. We sucked on our sourballs awhile, and then he said, "I never thought it would come to this, but the fact is, all I got left in life is lying in this bed listening to ball games. I don't know how it happened, but I woke up one day and I was old."

"You're not *that* old."

"I am *that* old, and I'm lying about like a slugabed. I should be up moving around a little." He nudged his sheets off with his feet and worked his legs over the side of the bed. "Give me your arm, boy."

I hopped up from the chair to help.

"All right," Gramps said as he stood up straight and leaned on me, "I'm steady now. Let's take this old body out for a spin."

We walked out to the bathroom, about ten feet away, which is as far as he ever walked anymore. But this time he wanted to go farther. He pointed down the hall, and I led him all the way to the back of the house with his hand on my shoulder. From there we could see out over Mom's vegetable garden and the rest of the yard. Gort was sprawled out there in the shade, taking his afternoon nap.

"That shed could use a coat of paint," Gramps said. "And those hemlock bushes need cutting back. You should be keeping an eye out around here for things that need tending to. You're old enough to pitch in. Don't *you* be a slugabed."

"Sure, Gramps," I said, even though I knew Dad wouldn't let me do anything important like painting the shed or pruning trees. He thought I'd make a mess of it, and he didn't have time to teach me to do it right. So I ended up not doing it at all.

After a minute Gramps shuffled back to his room. He stopped in front of the mirror over his bureau and hiked his nightshirt above his knees. He shook his head at what he saw.

"Look at these chicken legs. I can't believe they

belong to me. This mirror shows they're holding me up, so they must be mine. But they don't feel like mine. In my head, I still got legs that can ski down Tuckerman's Ravine."

"What's that?" I said.

"Tuckerman's Ravine is part of Mount Washington in the state of New Hampshire. It's shaped like a huge bowl. In the winter it fills up with snow, and then in the spring you hike up the side with your skis and shove yourself over the edge. It's about a three-hundred-foot drop."

"And you did that, skied off the ravine?"

"Sure I did. Every spring a group of us boys went up there. It's the fastest ride around, faster than the Thunderbolt at Willow Grove Park and a darn sight scarier than any roller coaster."

I wasn't sure whether to believe Gramps. He didn't exactly make things up, but he did sometimes enlarge them a little. I couldn't imagine the old body in front of me on skis at all, let alone blasting down any ravine.

"What do you think," Gramps said, dropping his nightshirt back over his legs, "that I spent my whole life in bed like this?"

It did seem that he'd been stuck in bed a lot, even before he moved in with us. First it was his broken hip, then the slipped disk in his back, now his bad heart.

"Don't confuse your years on earth with mine," he said. "I lived a lot of experiences before you were even born."

He stepped away from my arm. He seemed a little bit angry. Then he climbed back into bed all on his own.

Chapter 9
GRAMPS BEATS ME IN A RACE
(IT'S NOT AS BAD AS YOU THINK)

The next day Gramps was waiting for me to come into his room, with his legs over the side of the bed and his slippers on.

"I'm ready for another walk," he said.

"Sure, Gramps. Where to?"

"Don't be smart-alecky," he said and pointed down the hall again. There was only one way to go.

It seemed to me he was moving a little faster today, but like Mom always said, it's all relative. I've seen some inchworms crawling along faster than Gramps was moving. I imagined him and a worm racing down the hall. I'd have bet on the worm.

Sometimes with Gramps you had the spooky feeling he knew what you were thinking. When we got back to his room, he said, "All right, I've got my legs limbered up, I'm ready to race you."

"You couldn't beat a—" I caught myself just in time.

"A what?"

"Nothing. You couldn't beat me, that's all."

"I wager I could."

"Sure, Gramps."

"You think I'm kidding, you little whippersnapper? When did I ever kid you?"

"All the time."

"Maybe I do kid a lot, but I'm going to prove to you that I can beat you in a race." He sat down on the bed, and I helped lift his legs up and under the covers.

"You going to race me in bed?"

"Don't mock me, boy. I admit I'm—how do they say it these days, over the hill? In fact, I'm exactly seventy years older than you."

"And I'm practicing to join the track team when I get to junior high." Actually I was only thinking about practicing to go out for track. Mr. Deal, my gym teacher, said I might be good at it because I was thin and quick. Running seemed like the one sport a skinny kid like me could do.

"That so?" Gramps said. "You want to be the next Roger Bannister?"

"Who's that?"

"Why he's the English fellow who ran a mile in under four minutes a month ago, the first man to do that."

"Oh, yeah, then I want to be like him."

"That changes things. I was thinking you'd have to give me a five-yard lead. But if you're going to be a track runner like Roger Bannister, I'll probably need ten yards. We'll race the length of a football field."

"A ten-yard lead? I'd beat you if it was eighty yards."

Gramps raised his eyebrows in his "We'll see about that" look. "Hand me a piece of paper," he said.

I got him a pad and pencil from the nightstand. He drew a line across the page. "Here's the starting line," he said. He drew another line at the bottom. "And this is the finish." Then he wrote in a J at the starting line and a G about an inch ahead. "Is that a fair lead, or am I taking too much?"

"That's fair."

He handed me a pencil of my own. "Okay, now

the gun goes off—bang!" He started drawing a line from his G toward the finish, and I did from my J. "Whoa, slow down," he said. "Now, I can't move very fast, but I can still move some—I mean, I'm not dead, you grant me that?"

"Sure, you're not dead."

"And before you pass me, you have to catch up to me, right?"

"Yep."

"Well now, in any little bit of time where you're trying to catch me, I'm moving ahead, maybe a foot, maybe an inch." He moved his pencil a little. "Maybe even shorter, like a millimeter."

"Right."

"So there's no way of you ever going past me, is there?"

I didn't know how to answer. Gramps's drawing didn't fit very well with what I knew would happen in real life.

"How come I could beat you running on a track but not on paper?"

"Because words can muddy things up, that's why. You can convince somebody of anything, if you just know the right words to use."

"So you admit I'd beat you in a real race?"

He nodded. "Common sense says you would. You can have all the fancy ideas you want on paper, but you better test them to common sense." Gramps settled his head back on his pillows. "Think of it this way: Imagine there's a battle going on, like in that show we were watching the other night."

"The one where the Indians chased the cavalry?"

"That's it. Those soldiers tried to outrun the Indians' arrows. But we saw what happened, didn't we?"

"They got it in the back."

"Let that be a lesson to you," Gramps said, "words won't save you from an arrow headed your way."

It didn't seem to me I had to worry about an arrow headed for my back. But there might be a lot of other bad things I wanted to avoid in the world, and I figured I should be ready for them. Like giant mutant ants. They tried to take over the world in the movie *Them*, which I saw with Rudy before school let out. For months afterwards I was careful not to step on any ants

 on the sidewalk for fear of getting on their wrong side.

You wouldn't think you'd have to worry about little ants. But you never knew when they were going to turn mutant and take over the world.

"I could use another sourball," I said, because I always thought best about things while sucking on candy.

Gramps licked his lips. "I'll join you."

Chapter 10
WHY MY TONGUE TURNED GREEN

As the weeks passed in July, I felt like summer was racing on without me getting to do anything interesting. Rudy sent me an invitation to his birthday party, but Mom said definitely positively no, which meant there wasn't any use in complaining or arguing or whining or sulking about it.

Usually we went to Montgomery County Park to swim in the lake every other weekend, but not this year. She said that water was the worst place to pick up polio, and I didn't want that, did I? No, I didn't. But I sure didn't like doing nothing all summer, either.

Mom tried to keep me busy around the house with different projects. She bought me a big box of Lincoln Logs and let me build cabins and forts wherever I wanted, even in the living room. She had me sort through the utility drawer in the kitchen, which was full of stuff thrown in there for a couple of years, and let me keep any change I found. She paid me a quarter to take all of the cans and boxes out of the pantry, wipe down the shelves, and put everything back. I started to expect that each day she would have something else for me to do.

One morning she came into my room and dropped a big brown bag onto my bed before I had even gotten up.

"What's that?" I asked.

"Take a look."

I peeked into the bag and couldn't believe it. There were thousands of Green Stamps, enough to exchange for who knows what, maybe even one of those new Admiral color televisions like Joey's father bought. Dad said buying a color television was foolish because almost all the shows were black and white. He thought Joey's father was just showing off that he could spend $1,000 for something he couldn't even use. He said you could buy a whole car for as much as a color TV. I still wanted one.

Mom would go over the bridge to Abington to get gas at a station that gave Green Stamps. She didn't even mind paying twenty-two cents a gallon instead of twenty-one, because that just meant getting more stamps. She'd drive across town to the market that offered double stamps on Tuesdays, even if she could get all the things she needed at Blumhardt's uptown.

Dad said it was crazy rearranging your life around getting Green Stamps. He said the stores that gave them out with every purchase charged more, so you only thought you were getting something for free.

"Maybe so, maybe not," Mom said, which is about as close as she ever got to telling him he was wrong.

She handed me a dozen empty S&H books. "You paste all of these stamps in for me, and I'll make sure you get to pick a gift for yourself from the catalog."

"Like a new bike?" I said.

"I don't think we have enough stamps for that, Jesse, but something nice."

"Okay," I said, "you've got a deal."

I got started after breakfast. I thought I'd be done by lunch. But after licking and pasting and licking and pasting for hours, I'd hardly made a dent in the bag.

My tongue turned green, and I was feeling a little sick. I tried getting Gort to help me, but when I held out a strip of stamps for him to lick, it stuck to his tongue and he took off running. I didn't see him the rest of the day.

So I dumped the stamps out on my bed and started looking for double-wides that would fill the book up faster. I never found any. It was all little strips of ones, on and on and on.

Mom poked her head into my bedroom every once in a while and said, "Do them neatly now, and make sure you count right. We don't want S&H to think we're trying to cheat them." She spoke about S&H like it was a person we knew, not some company that gave out stamps.

By midafternoon I didn't care what S&H thought. My stomach felt nauseous, like the time I ate half a box of Kellogg's Sugar Smacks, which Mom said was candy masquerading as cereal.

I guess it was something in the glue that made me sick. I should have used a sponge to wet the stamps, like Mom said. I didn't care if I ever saw a Green Stamp again. I didn't even care about picking out something for myself from the catalog. I shoved the remaining tangle of stamps back in the bag and marched into the kitchen. I had to get out of the house into the fresh air.

"Can't I *please* go to the movies today, Mom? *Invaders from Mars* is playing, and I'm pretty sure it's definitely the last week at the Hiway. I haven't seen a movie for months."

She didn't say no right away, which was a good sign.

"It's awful hot out to be walking all the way to the theater."

"It's only uptown," I said. Jenkintown was so small you could walk anywhere and not get overheated.

"You're not meeting anybody there, are you?"

"No, Mom. I'll be by myself."

She put down her mixing bowl and gave me a hug. "You understand I haven't been keeping you inside as punishment, Jesse. It's just polio has gotten us all a little crazy."

"You go out," I said, "and Dad's off selling brushes."

"You know that polio hits children worse than adults. Besides, parents have to go out in the summer to make a living. Children don't."

"I'll be very very careful," I said. "I already missed *Bwana Devil*, and that was 3-D. Ricky said they gave out special glasses and all."

"I know you've missed a lot this summer," she said as she brushed back my hair. I didn't like her doing it, but I let her since I was asking for something. "So I guess you can go this one time. But be back by dinner. We're having pea and Brussels sprout pie."

"What?"

"Just kidding," she said, giving me a kiss on the top of the head. Then she pulled a dollar from her apron. "Have fun, and don't eat too much popcorn."

Chapter 11
THE HEAD INSIDE THE GLASS

The Hiway Theater was half full of kids, and every one of them seemed to be with someone else. I felt stupid being alone. I figured they were all looking at me, thinking, *He must not have any friends.* So when I went to the popcorn machine, I bought two bags so that it would look like I was taking one back to a buddy. Of course, that meant that I'd have to eat two bags.

The older kids sat in the back row making out. They were all ninth and tenth graders. I started down the aisle to find a seat and a kid ran into me, which sent my popcorn flying. "Watch it, spaz," he said, as if I'd bumped into him.

That frosted me. "Get bent," I said, but not so he could really hear me.

"What'd you say?"

"Nothing." I know that sounds really wimpy of

me. I should have given him a knuckle sandwich and sent him into orbit. But he was bigger than me, and I wasn't any Charles Atlas, at least not yet.

I hurried around the kid and went up to the front row, which was empty. From there I had to lean my head way back to see the screen, but at least nobody would bother me. I was doing what Mom told me—staying away from other kids. Of course, the popcorn made me so thirsty I had to keep running out to the water fountain, since I didn't have money for a soda.

There were three cartoons before the movie, and my favorite was Bugs Bunny in *Devil May Hare*. It had a character I'd never seen before—Taz. Taz had a big belly and big mouth and short arms and legs, like a Tasmanian devil. Bugs looks up "Tasmanian devil" in  the dictionary and finds that it's an animal from Tasmania, which is part of Australia.

When Taz opens his jaws to have a rabbit meal, Bugs says that he's so skinny he wouldn't be worth the trouble to eat. He suggests something with more meat on it. Taz likes the sound of that, and Bugs tricks him into eating a bubblegum chicken and an inflatable pig.

After the cartoons, the curtain closed for a minute and then opened slowly, which meant it was time for the main feature. First, of course, came the National Anthem. Everybody in the theater stood up, and I put my hand on my chest as the big American flag waved on the screen. I heard a few kids behind me laughing and throwing candy, and I thought it was good Dad wasn't there. He would have gone ape on them for disrespecting the flag.

Invaders from Mars was about the coolest movie I ever saw. A kid named David wakes up in the middle of the night and sees a flying saucer land outside his window. But nobody believes him because he's only twelve years old. His dad finally goes to investigate, and when he comes back he starts acting all weird. David sees a scar on the back of his neck and figures out what happened: good old dad has been taken over by the aliens. Next thing his mother goes alien, too.

The kid runs off to tell the cops and gets locked up in jail because the police chief has been taken over also. Finally David finds one adult, Dr. Blake, who will

listen. She gets the military to investigate, and David goes with them to the UFO site. The ground swallows them up, which leads them to the bug-eyed aliens. The head guy is just that—a head! He's sitting inside a glass jar, with tentacles sticking out of him, like a giant insect.

I won't spoil it by telling the ending, but you can probably guess that the kid gets rescued and the aliens are blown to kingdom come. From the poster outside the Hiway, I thought the giant aliens with the dragonfly heads would be scary. But I swear that when one of them turned around, I saw the zipper going up the back of his green costume. It's hard to get scared about something in a costume if you aren't a little kid anymore.

What did give me nightmares for weeks were the parents. After the aliens took them over, they became strange and mean. They looked like the same people, but inside they were different. I began wondering about Dad's scar, and whether he really got it in the war like he said, or if maybe aliens had gotten to him. You heard about flying saucers landing in the country all the time.

Usually it was out West where there weren't as many people. I'd read amazing stories of UFOs in *Amazing Stories* magazine. Some people said the aliens took them up into their spaceships and did weird tests on them.

It seemed possible that aliens had taken over Dad's body when he was away traveling for his job. What I couldn't figure out was, why him? It wasn't like he was a scientist working on the hydrogen bomb or anything. He sold brushes.

I had always thought I'd know a monster when I saw one. But after watching *Invaders from Mars*, I wasn't so sure.

Chapter 12
THE WORST DAY OF MY LIFE (SO FAR)

The matinee didn't get out until 4:58, which meant I couldn't get home by five o'clock even if I were Roger Bannister. It would take me ten minutes running. Walking, more like twenty. I figured if I was already going to get in trouble for being late, I didn't want to get it worse for showing up all sweaty.

So I took my time and even stopped outside Shelton's Aquarium for a few minutes to watch the fancy rainbow fish and puffers swimming in the fish tanks in the window. I didn't have time to go inside to see the plain old guppies and goldfish, which were the only ones I could afford. The last ones I'd bought all died, which is why Mom wouldn't let me get any more until I turned twelve. She was expecting I'd be more responsible then. I didn't see how I could be irresponsible at age eleven and 364 days and suddenly become responsible the next day at age twelve. Mom said it *would* be a miracle.

When I got home, she was scooping out her casserole. She put a plate of it on Gramps's tray along with a large sugar cookie. I'd saved him a half box of Raisinettes from the movies, so he'd have two desserts tonight. I knew he'd love that.

"You're late, Jesse," Mom said when she heard the screen door shut behind me. "Take this to your grandfather while it's still hot and then wash up for supper."

"Sure," I said.

The casserole looked like her macaroni-tomato-onion-ground-beef concoction, which she made without checking a recipe. She just tossed things in, which made it kind of scary to eat because you never knew what taste was going to land on your tongue. She added whatever was left open in the refrigerator from the last meal or a spice that was almost used up. It seemed like something I'd do with my chemistry set—throw everything together and see what happened.

"Didn't you say goodbye to your grandfather before you left this afternoon?"

"I was going to," I said, "but I was late for the movie."

"He was calling for you. He said he had a message."

"What message?"

"I don't know. I suppose he'll tell you now."

I walked up the stairs just like Gramps told me, looking straight ahead rather than at the tray. I didn't spill a drop of his coffee, which Mom had filled to the brim.

At his door I knocked with my head, but he didn't answer. I knocked again.

"Hey, Gramps," I said. "President Eisenhower's downstairs. He wants to give you a medal for beating me in the race the other day."

Gramps didn't answer. I figured he was listening to a ball game, with the radio pressed up against his ear. So I nudged open the door with my foot and walked in.

There he was as always, sitting straight up in bed.

"Hi, Gramps," I said. "Sorry I didn't say good-bye to you today, but I had to hurry out to see this really neat movie. You would have liked it, especially the aliens with the zippers up their backs."

I set the tray on his table and looked at him. His

eyes were really wide, like he'd seen something that frightened him so much he wouldn't close them for fear it would sneak back. I thought of the invaders from Mars.

"You okay, Gramps?"

I reached over and poked him in the shoulder, which I had to do sometimes when he was napping. He keeled over sideways. His head bounced on the mattress. I didn't know what to think. This was scarier than any creepy movie.

I turned to run and knocked his dinner to the floor, spilling the messy casserole all over. I started to clean it up but then thought, *Why am I doing that? Who cares about the rug?* I had to get help.

"Mom! Mom!" I called, but she didn't answer. I dashed down the hall and down the steps. She was carrying plates to the kitchen table. "It's Gramps," I said. "He fell over on his bed."

"Is he okay?"

"No, no, he looks really bad, like he's . . . You know."

She grabbed the phone on the wall and called the police. Then she went flying up the stairs faster than I'd ever seen her move. I started after her, but she told me to go out front and watch for the ambulance.

Chapter 13
GRAMPS'S SECRET MESSAGE

It all happened so fast. The ambulance guys came running up the porch and into the house. I pointed them to the upstairs, then waited. I didn't want to see what was happening up there, but I did, too. It's like at the movies when you know the scary part's coming so you cover your eyes but then peek through your fingers.

I walked from the living room through the dining room to the kitchen, trying not to think about Gramps. But everywhere there was something to remind me—like on the hall cabinet, the little Gort dog he made out of solder. Or in the magazine rack, the book he gave me on the famous gangster, Dutch Schultz, who Gramps actually met one time. Most of all like on the mantel over the fireplace, the picture of my grandfather sitting on the railing at the Atlantic City boardwalk, eyeing the girls passing by. It was strange thinking that the young guy in the picture was the same as the old man upstairs.

In a few minutes they came down carrying him on a stretcher, with a breathing mask over his mouth. They pushed past me and were out the door. Mom told me to stay in the house, then jumped in the back of the ambulance with him.

As the ambulance disappeared down the street, I had that sinking feeling of seeing something happening that you can't change no matter how much you wish or pray it to be different. I hated the idea that the last time I might ever see Gramps would be strapped to a stretcher, being carried away to a hospital. He would hate that, too.

I went upstairs to his room. It was a mess. The sheets to his bed were thrown on the floor. The coffee was spilled all over the rug. The goosehead lamp he read by was knocked over. I bent down to pick it up and saw a piece of paper with my name on it. I opened it up and read:

" Remember the radio! Love forever, your grandfather."

The words were blurry, as if his hand was shaking when he wrote it. I knew this was it, his secret message. I couldn't help bawling thinking about how I might never see him again. I might have even saved him if I just hadn't gone to the stupid movie.

I smeared away the tears with my arm and saw the radio on his bed. I picked it up and pressed it to the side of my face. It still felt warm, like from his face.

I took the radio to my room and lay down on my bed. Gort jumped up next to me and began licking the tears off my cheeks. He knew something was wrong. He'd never seen me cry before.

I settled him down and then stared at the wall where the rapping always came when Gramps wanted me. I tried to make that rapping happen again with all the force of my mind. But I couldn't reverse time to yesterday or any other day.

Still, I thought maybe there was a chance he'd come home again. After all, they had the breathing mask on him. He must have been alive when he left. And people went to hospitals to get better, not to die.

I wasn't one to pray a lot, except before bed. It didn't seem right to be always asking God for things for yourself when there were so many other people worse off needing his attention. Gramps taught me that. But this was a special case. I wasn't praying for me, but for him.

So I promised God that if he let my grandfather live, I wouldn't ever try smoking again. But that wasn't really much of a sacrifice for me, since I got sick the time I took one of Dad's Camels and puffed on it for a few minutes. I suppose I should have tried a weaker cigarette for my first time, but I liked the camel on the pack.

Then I promised God I wouldn't swear anymore, even small swears like—well, I can't say them because I promised. That still didn't sound like enough, though. If you were asking for a big favor, you needed to make a big sacrifice.

Suddenly I sat up in bed. I came up with the best promise ever: NO COMPLAINING. I, Jesse James MacLean, would hereby promise not to complain for the whole next year if God would just make Gramps well again. I wouldn't complain about mowing the lawn, or carrying the trash to the curb, or doing my homework on a Sunday afternoon, or . . . The list could go on and on. I wouldn't even complain about Dad, whenever he came back.

If that didn't impress God, nothing would!

Chapter 14
"OH, PANCHO"

God must have had more important things to take care of that day. Mom called me from the hospital to say that Gramps "didn't make it." At first I didn't know what that meant. Then she said he *had* lived a good long life, and I knew.

She told me I should be proud because I had made his last weeks on Earth very special. I made his life special? I thought Gramps had made my life special. I guess sometimes you don't know how important you are to other people.

I couldn't stand being inside the house alone. I ran out into our backyard and started spinning with my arms out to the side, as if they were wings that would lift me off the ground and set me down somewhere else far away. I got so dizzy that I fell to the grass and stared up into the bluest evening sky I'd ever seen. Everything seemed to be the most that it had ever been—the grass under me the softest I ever felt it, the clouds above me the brightest white.

I wondered where Gramps was, up there floating toward Heaven? I squinted at the clouds, and I think I saw him. There was a round ball at the top that looked like a head, and thin puffs of white on either side. I imagined that was him, skiing down Tuckerman's Ravine like he said. I figured Gramps would be happy forever if he could ski in Heaven. Of course, he'd want to be able to hear the Phillies games, too.

I couldn't stop thinking about him the next day and the next. No one had ever died around me before. The only dying I'd seen was on Westerns, and I never cried watching anyone get shot on TV. That's what was supposed to happen to cowboys.

I didn't feel like watching any of my favorite shows, and when I did they reminded me of him. Like Cosmo, the old guy who moved into the haunted house in *Topper*. He had the same grumpy look as Gramps. And like at the end of *The Cisco Kid*, when Pancho says, "Oh, Cisco," and Cisco says, "Oh, Pancho," before they ride off together. Well, that's what Gramps and I would say to each other when I was going off to bed. I was The Cisco Kid and he was my best buddy, Pancho.

I thought I had cried myself out after two days, but when I walked down the hall I started crying again. I stopped in front of his door and knocked with my head, just like I was carrying his tray.

"Look out your window, Gramps, there's a limousine out front to take us to *Ted Mack's Amateur Hour* show in New York. I'm going to do yo-yo tricks, and you can challenge Mr. Mack to a race."

Gramps had promised to take me to New York some time, but that was before he got sick. He said we could ride up and down the elevator in the Empire State Building all day if I wanted.

"Grand-daddio?" I said, which is something I never called him before, but I was sure he'd like it.

He didn't answer.

"Oh, Pancho," I said. "Oh, Pancho."

I waited to hear "Oh, Cisco" one more time, but his room was silent.

Chapter 15
SAVED FROM GRACE

I began remembering all kinds of things about Gramps, like what happened last Christmas.

When relatives came at holidays, everyone would hold hands around the dinner table, and the youngest would be called on to say grace. Most times that was me, and I hated it. Sometimes I stuttered. When I did get the words out, they sounded all squeaky. I only knew one grace, which was: "Thank You for the world so sweet, thank You for the food we eat, thank You for the birds that sing, thank You, God, for everything. Amen." That was a little kid's nursery rhyme, not something an eleven-year-old would say.

But while I'd definitely grown out of being a little kid, sometimes I didn't know what I'd grown into yet. I wasn't an adult and didn't really want to be, especially if it meant doing something like selling brushes.

On Christmas Day Mom and Dad's families

came to dinner. You'd think out of nineteen people, seven of them kids, one of them would be younger than me. Nope. My cousin Patsy, born two months after me, a fact that I had checked and double-checked with Mom, stayed home with the German measles. I was stuck doing grace again, and I hadn't planned anything new.

Just as Dad finished carving the turkey, Mom said, "Now who's the youngest here? I guess that's you, Jesse. Will you say grace?"

It wasn't a real question, not where you could actually answer yes or no. With aunts and uncles and cousins all sitting there looking at me, I couldn't say, "I don't really want to say grace tonight." So I coughed a few times, stalling, like I'd learned to do in class when I needed a few seconds to come up with an answer. I thought about just winging it, saying whatever came to my mind, like I'd heard adults do at other people's houses. But I couldn't think of anything.

"Go ahead," Dad said.

Just then Gramps spoke up. "Why is it the youngest always gets the pleasure of saying grace? How come it's never the oldest who's asked to do the honor?"

I felt a foot tap mine under the table. When I looked across, Gramps winked at me.

"What do you say, boy? How about letting me say our thanks tonight?"

I looked to the head of the table and Dad nodded.

"Sure, Gramps," I said, "you can say it, if you really want to."

We all bowed our heads. "Our Father, we're sitting here on Your Son's birthday with a table full of good things before us. Bless this turkey that gave its life so we can eat. Bless this family, including the relatives who came so far to be together with us this day. Help us not to forget the families that are broken up and the people in this world who don't even have homes to live in."

Here Gramps took a breath, and I sneaked open my eyes. Everyone's head was bowed, like it was supposed to be. How come adults were never curious enough to peek to see who else was peeking? Even the other kids' eyes were closed. That made me ashamed that I was the only one looking. I shut my eyes.

"I could go on for a while," Gramps continued, "but the gravy and biscuits are hot, and I think You get the idea of how thankful we are. Amen."

"Amen!" I said louder than I ever had. Now *that* was a grace, and the best thing about it was that I didn't have to say it. Gramps saved me.

He was always doing things like that. When I spent two weeks' allowance on comic books, forgetting that Mother's Day was coming up, it was Gramps who understood the temptation to spend all of my allowance on a *Tom Corbett, Space Cadet* issue from May 1952 with the Space Cadet Pledge on the inside cover. He loaned me the money to buy Mom a present. And when my new O-Boy Whistler yo-yo flew off my finger while I was practicing round-the-world, which knocked my glass of grape Kool-Aid onto my bedroom rug, I called him. He told me to use bleach to get out the stain without Mom knowing. When the bleach left a worse-looking mark than the Kool-Aid, I called him back, and he said just to move my chair over the stain. That worked perfectly.

I thanked him each time he helped me. But when had I actually done anything important for Gramps besides carrying up his meals every day? Now was my opportunity. I would remember the radio.

Chapter 16
LICKING IVORY (DRY YOUR TONGUE FIRST)

Three days after Gramps died, Mom stood behind me in the bathroom, helping me to get the knot in my tie straight. "Times like this I miss your father," she said. "I wish I knew how to reach him."

"I don't," I said.

He'd been gone eight days already and had only called once, before Gramps died. She always looked out the window when a car slowed down in front of our house, thinking it might be the Buick turning into our driveway.

"A boy needs a father," she said.

"I don't care if he ever comes back," I said. "I wish he wouldn't."

She looked at me with a fierce expression, and I knew I'd said too much. Sometimes when a mean thought goes through your head, it's better to zip your mouth closed.

"That's a terrible thing to say," she said, "especially on a day like this." You never know when you're going to lose someone."

"I don't care if we lose *him*."

You'd think a kid would learn when to shut up, but not me.

Mom pulled away, leaving my tie crooked. "I didn't teach you to disrespect your father," she said. "Go get the Ivory."

If I took back what I'd said, I had a chance of escaping the soap punishment. But I didn't want to take it back. I meant it.

I walked to the bathroom as slowly as I could. It must have taken me five minutes to come back with a new bar of Ivory. I hoped something else had occurred to Mom to do, but she was waiting for me in the bathroom. I handed her the soap. She tore down the wrapper halfway and handed it back. I knew the drill. I held the bar out in front of my mouth and took a little lick.

She shook her head. "The whole tongue. You have to learn not to think such terrible things."

I didn't see how the soap punishment would change what I thought, only what I said. But I didn't tell her that.

I licked my tongue on a towel a couple of times to get it as dry as possible. A dry tongue doesn't pick up the soap as easily, which I'd learned from Rudy, who got the soap punishment a lot more than I did. At least Mom didn't run the Ivory under the water first, like Rudy's mother.

I licked the bar again. This time a thin film of soap spread over my taste buds.

"Five good licks," she said, "and then it will be over with."

I took a second long lick, and a third and a fourth. I held my tongue out so the air would dry it.

"Come on, hurry now so we can have a little lunch before we leave."

"Lunch?" I said, although it came out sounding more like "Unth?" It would take me hours to get the soap taste out of my mouth. I'd probably be blowing bubbles at the funeral. The last thing I wanted to do was eat. I brought the soap toward my mouth. Instead of licking, this time I just dragged the bar quickly across the length of my tongue. "At oh-ey?" I asked.

"Yes," she said, "that's okay."

Chapter 17
CAUGHT WITH MY HAND IN THE COFFIN

Mom drove us to the church in Gramps's 1949 Ford, which he called Henry. Henry was older than our Buick, which didn't have a name. Dad took that one on his trips. "Fords aren't the fanciest cars," my grandfather used to say, "but they run and run and run."

We were late getting to his old church in Glenside because my mother never had a sense of direction. Driving to places was something she always counted on Dad to take care of.

The line for viewing Gramps's body stretched out the door and down the steps. The minister spotted us and said we should go to the front, but my mother waved him off. "We're in no hurry," she said.

The people ahead of us talked about the drought we were having. A couple of the ushers were saying how the Phillies might still have a chance this year if the pitching held up. I wished Gramps could have heard that. He would have had a fine conversation at his own funeral.

Everyone nodded or waved to us. A few women came up and took Mom's hand and said, "It's sad, but it's for the best at his age."

That seemed stupid to me. How could it be for the best when your grandfather dies and you don't have the chance to say goodbye? One of the women patted me on the head, which knocked down one side of my crewcut. I didn't like that either.

We shuffled closer to the casket. Mom said I didn't have to look in if I didn't want to. She didn't know I did have to look, and more than that. Gramps had made me swear to a secret that I'd kept for the whole six weeks he lived with us. He wanted to be buried with his transistor radio.

I didn't understand when he told me. What would he need a radio for if he was dead?

"You never know how things are going to work in the next world," he said. "I want to be ready in case I can get the ball games."

"Why don't you ask Mom or somebody to put the radio in with you?" I asked him.

"Because they'd think I'm just a foolish old man. You're the only one I can trust to do it."

So there I was, Gramps's only hope, approaching the casket. Mom stopped for a moment, said some words I couldn't hear, and pulled me on.

I dug my heels in and shook my hand out of hers. "I didn't see him," I said.

"Go ahead then, say goodbye to your grandfather. He loved you dearly."

I turned back to the coffin, stepped up on my toes, and there was Gramps spread out like a fallen-over wax figure painted to look real. I felt guilty for thinking this, but he looked better dead than alive. His face was clear of the red splotches on his cheeks that made him look like some old-time cowboy who drank whiskey all day. He'd been shaved close, too, straight up to his sideburns and all over his neck. I figured he must be dead if he let them shave his sideburns that high. He always left them long and bushy. He used to let me touch them when I was a real little kid.

I brushed away the tears with my sleeve and remembered his instructions: *Take the radio from inside your jacket and put it under the blanket next to my arm.*

I peeked over my shoulder. Behind me, my great-aunt Sarah was crying into her handkerchief, and everyone was either comforting her or talking to my mother. I took this as my opportunity to slip the little radio over the edge of the casket.

Before I pulled back out, I couldn't resist touching Gramps's face. It didn't feel like skin at all, but like some old paint that had hardened in its can in the garage.

"God help us!"

I whirled around, and there was Aunt Sarah jabbing her cane in the air at me as my hand came out of the casket.

"What on earth are you doing, Jesse?" Mom said as she dragged me away.

"Nothing," I said in my most innocent voice. No matter what she thought or how many bars of Ivory soap she made me lick, I wouldn't tell her about the transistor radio. It was the least I could do for Gramps.

Chapter 18
JUMP? HOW HIGH, SIR?

I'd just gotten used to Dad being gone that summer when a car drove up to the garage, and I heard the horn.

"It's him," Mom said. She sounded so relieved that I felt guilty for wishing he'd gotten knocked in the head so he couldn't remember where he lived, or been beamed up to a spaceship by Martians who needed Fuller brushes. I've always wondered whether other kids wish for bad stuff to happen to their parents sometimes, but I never asked any of my buddies. I guess I didn't want to find out I was the only one with such terrible thoughts.

"Watch what you say," Mom instructed me as she put on lipstick in the hall mirror, "and do what he asks."

Asks? Dad never asked me to do anything. He always told me what do, like he was the captain and I was the private in his own personal army. He told me once, "If I say jump, don't ask why, just, 'How high?'"

Sometimes he actually did come out to the driveway where I was oiling my bike and yell, "Jump, mister." I'd stand up and say, "How high, Captain?" and he'd say, "I can't hear you." So I'd have to yell, "How high, SIR?" Then he'd say twelve inches and I'd jump as high as I could straight up. He'd nod and then leave me alone. When he did this I felt like a dog he was training, except he never gave me any treats for obeying.

Mom opened the front door, and Dad came through, carrying his suitcase in one hand and his samples case in the other.

"Oh, Jack," she said, "I'm so glad you're home. Something terrible has happened. My father passed away."

Dad looked upstairs for a second, as if trying to imagine that there was nobody up there now. Then he put his arms around her. "Your father died?"

She nodded. "I didn't know where you were. I didn't have any way to reach you. We buried him two days ago."

"I'm so sorry, honey," he said, stroking her hair.

"I wish I had been here for you." He actually sounded very sincere.

"I knew he didn't have long to live," she said. "Still, it's an awful shock."

"He did a lot in his life," Dad said. "He lived every minute."

Mom started crying suddenly, as if she just couldn't hold it in any longer. I hadn't seen her cry at all since Gramps died, not even at the funeral. Maybe she just needed somebody to cry to.

I would have let her cry on me all she wanted, if I had just known.

Chapter 19
ME, A GOPHER (SORT OF)

Dad's first day back from a trip was usually okay, because he tried to make up for being away. He was especially on his good behavior this time since Gramps had died. He had Mom write down all the things that needed fixing. Then he sent me running for tools or towels or lubricating oil, whatever the job needed. He called me his gopher, which I didn't understand because dogs were the only animals I knew that fetched things. Gophers just dug holes in the ground.

I said to him, "Shouldn't you call me your hound dog or retriever or something, 'cause gophers don't go for things?"

When he got done laughing he said, "You're my *go-for*—you *go for* things—you're not a g-o-p-h-e-r." As usual, I felt awful stupid in front of him.

Sometimes when he was doing a job Dad needed

an extra hand, meaning mine, and I listened carefully so that I'd do exactly as he wanted. I even wore the Brooklyn Dodgers cap he bought me for playing Little League. It was his favorite team. He didn't know I always sat on the bench. The coach said he was afraid to put me in because I might get hit in the face with a ball. He was probably right.

Anyway, they stopped the season early because of polio. All three of the Michaelson boys, who were our outfield, caught the disease after going go-karting one hot night. Bobby Michaelson was the fastest kid on the team, until he landed in a wheelchair.

So with my Dodgers cap on, I was helping Dad fix the stuck front window. I was holding it up while he finished checking the new ropes he'd just put in.

"Okay, let it go," he said. I know absolutely for sure that he said, "Let it go."

"Righto," I said and loosened my grip on the window. The ropes seemed to hold, and I smiled proudly at him even though I had helped only a little. A cool wind blew in from the porch, meaning a thunderstorm was on its way. Dad started to smile—pretty unusual for him—but then there was a quick snapping sound, and the window crashed down on his fingers.

"My hand!" he yelled in a voice I had never heard from him before. His eyes started watering. Was my father going to cry? "Pull it up!" he said. I tried to, but the sash was out of line and wouldn't budge. He took a deep breath and closed his eyes. "Get your mother." I froze, staring at his thick right hand swelling up. When he opened his eyes and saw me still there he yelled, "Go!"

I ran through the dining room and kitchen and pushed open the screen door and jumped off the steps into the backyard. Mom was hanging wet socks on the clothesline, a chore she often asked me to help her with. I sure wish she had that day. A wooden clothespin bobbed between her lips.

"It's Dad," I said. "Come quick." I grabbed her arm and pulled her into the house, through the kitchen and the dining room, into the living room. I pointed at the window. Dad wasn't there.

She said, "If this is some game of yours, young man."

"It's not a game, it's not a game," I said, twirling around, trying to understand what was happening.

Maybe I'd just imagined the window falling on him. I wanted to believe that. Then a stream of curses came tumbling down from the upstairs bathroom. In a moment my father stomped down the stairs with his right hand wrapped in a towel.

Mom ran up to him. "What in Heaven's name?"

"That fool," he said, and I was sure he was going to say "fool window," but he said, "That fool boy let the window drop on my hand."

She turned on me with eyes that seemed to be seeing someone else—not her favorite son, as she always called me, a small joke between us since I was their only child. She believed him, and I couldn't for the life of me understand why.

Chapter 20
OF DEADEYES AND DOPES

I finally figured out the one thing that Dad and I shared: the cowboy gene. We'd both watch any of them that was on television, even the ones we didn't really like. We sat next to each other on the couch with our feet up on the hassock. Sometimes he snuck in popcorn, even though we weren't supposed to eat anything in the living room. It was his rule, so I guess that's why we could break it.

We agreed that Gene Autry was pretty dopey. I said I bet even his horse Champion got sick of him singing all the time, and that made Dad laugh. He said that Roy Rogers looked like he was dressed up to go to a square dance and didn't want to get his "perty" clothes messed up. Then there was Sky King, who piloted a plane instead of riding a horse, which I guess means he wasn't a real cowboy. He flew around rescuing his niece,

Penny, who kept getting into dangerous situations. Sometimes we wished he would just leave her in the cave or pit or wherever she was, because she was pretty irritating.

We both liked Hopalong Cassidy, who wore all black, including a black hat, even though he was a good guy. For some reason, his show wasn't on any more. Kit Carson was a deadeye scout, but Dad thought Annie Oakley was the best sharpshooter of them all. Each week she tried to clean up Diablo, which was a rough sort of cowboy town. We liked the way she could ride a horse and do trick shooting. Dad said not many men could do that.

One night we watched Westerns so late that I fell

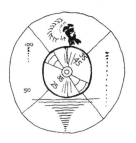 asleep next to him on the sofa. He woke me up at midnight to hear the National Anthem being played, meaning the broadcast was over for the day. I saluted, like he did. Then we just sat there and stared at the test pattern, with an Indian chief on top.

It was as if a kind of spell had come over Dad and me

that night that neither of us wanted to break. I couldn't remember being that close to him for so long since I was a little kid sitting in his lap.

Mom finally came downstairs in her bathrobe. She looked at the TV, then at us. "What on earth are you two doing?" she said. "That test pattern's not going to change, you know."

Dad started laughing and I did, too. "I guess we've been looking at this box so long we got hypnotized," he said.

Mom turned off the television. "You'd think you two had been drinking beer all night, as silly as you're acting." She picked up our soda glasses and smelled them to make sure we weren't.

I didn't expect that things would change between Dad and me just because we had one good night together. I still knew deep down that I wasn't the boy he wished he had, whether or not we shared the cowboy gene.

Chapter 21
DUCK AND COVER

The next day Dad told Mom and me to meet him at three p.m. sharp in the kitchen for a family conference, that he had something important to show us.

"What's a family conference?" I asked her, since we'd never had one before.

"It's where the whole family gets together to discuss something."

"What're we discussing?"

"I don't know," she said. "We'll have to wait for your father to come up from the cellar."

We watched the hour hand hit three, then go past. Mom made a cup of Ovaltine for me and tea for herself. I couldn't understand how anybody would choose to drink tea. It was bad enough that you had to when you were sick.

"We're ready, Jack," Mom called down the steps a few times.

Dad finally came upstairs, with a rolled-up paper in his hands.

"Okay," he said, "give me some room."

We moved away our cups, and he opened up what looked like a drawing that wasn't filled in.

"What is it, Dad?"

"This," he said, "is our answer to the Russians."

Mom poked him in the side. "I didn't know they had asked us a question."

Dad looked at her with a fake smile. "It's no joke that the Russians have the hydrogen bomb now. Their missiles can reach our cities in a couple of hours."

"He's right, Mom. They showed us this film at school called *Duck and Cover*. That's what you're supposed to do if an H-bomb goes off, duck under a desk or table and cover your head, like Bert."

"Bert?"

"Yeah, Bert the Turtle. He's in the film."

"We're taking advice from Bert the Turtle now?" Mom said.

"No," Dad said, "we're taking the advice of the Civil Defense Agency. These are blueprints on how to build—"

"A fallout shelter," I shouted. "That's what it is."

"Right you are, buddy. This is a design for a do-it-yourself fallout shelter to protect our family. It's eight by ten feet, with shelves for food and water. I'm going to build it in the corner of the basement so there'll be two sides already protected by earth. All I have to do is put up two more walls out of concrete blocks and reinforce the ceiling with plywood and bricks."

Dad moved the salt and pepper shakers to the top ends of the paper to keep it from rolling down. He looked as excited as I'd seen him about anything, and I was, too.

"So, what do you think?" he said.

Mom looked at the drawings, then at Dad, then back to the drawings.

"Where would the facilities be?"

"The facilities?" Dad asked.

"A toilet—or would we have to hold it the whole time we're in there?"

"Very funny," Dad said. "I'm figuring on putting in a chemical toilet like they use in the army . . . behind a curtain."

"Sounds lovely," Mom said. "And air? What do we do for air, sealed up in a concrete bunker?"

"There're ways of ventilating," Dad said. "I just haven't gotten to that yet."

Mom pointed at the drawings. "And this is going to protect us from an H-bomb dropped on the house?"

"No, of course not, we'll be blown to smithereens if that happens. An H-bomb is seven hundred times more powerful than the A-bomb we dropped on Hiroshima. But the thing is, Jenkintown isn't important enough to be a target. The Russians will bomb Philadelphia because of the Navy Yard. It's the fallout we have to watch out for, the gamma rays."

Mom leaned over the drawings. On the side was written: "632 bricks, 400 12-inch-thick concrete blocks, 2 lbs. #10 nails, 10 pounds mortar."

"You're going to seal us up in an eight-by-ten room for how long?"

"Two weeks should be enough for the radiation to fall out of the air. Then it would be safe to come out."

"Two weeks?" Mom said, rolling her eyes. She had a way of doing that that made her eyes look like they were going to fall out. "I'll take my chances with the radiation over living like a mole."

Not me. I thought the fallout shelter was the best idea Dad ever had, and I was sure he'd let me help him build it.

"There's enough room for the three of us," he said. "You'll be comfortable."

The *three* of us? "There's four of us," I said. "Remember Gort?" At the sound of his name, Gort poked his nose out from under the table and rested his chin on my knee.

Mom and Dad looked at each other in a way I knew meant I wasn't going to like what was coming.

"I'm afraid the shelter's not big enough for a dog," Dad said.

"Then you have to make it bigger," I said. "You said the shelter was to protect the family. Gort's part of the family."

"He's a dog. He wouldn't like being cooped up in a little room for two weeks."

"He'd like it better than dying from the radiation."

"Where's he going to relieve himself? We couldn't let him out of the shelter to go in the yard. He's not a cat who can use a litter box."

I couldn't answer this question. I had never thought about how Gort relieved himself. I just opened the back door and he ran out to the strip of ivy and did his business. A few minutes later he came running back in.

"Your father's right," Mom said. "You see that, don't you, Jesse?"

Yes, I saw that. It would be pretty hard to keep a dog inside a small room with us for two weeks. Still, I leaned down to Gort's ear and whispered so they couldn't hear me: "Don't worry, boy. I won't go in the shelter without you."

Chapter 22
GAMES YOU PLAY WHEN YOU'RE SICK

She said I'd caught a summer cold. On a hot sticky Friday morning, she propped me up on the sofa in the living room where she could check on me as she did her housework. She took my temperature every two hours, and it kept climbing about a half a degree each time. She said if it hit 101 she would call Dr. Metz. I was awful thirsty, so she brought me a tall glass of ginger ale, which she insisted I let sit for ten minutes so the fizz would die down.

I tried to sleep as much as I could, but by the afternoon my legs started aching and I felt like throwing up. When I told Mom that, she said I probably had the summer flu, which was worse than a summer cold, but I'd get over it soon enough. She set a bucket next to the sofa in case I had to heave before making it to the bathroom. Then she made Lipton tea and stood over me to make sure I drank it. I said the tea would make me throw up, but she just said, "Drink." She spread Vicks VapoRub on my chest, then fixed a towel over my head so that I had to breathe in the fumes. "Vicks will cure what ails you," she said.

I wanted to be cured as fast as possible because I never knew when Dad would come home from his trip and start building the fallout shelter. He had bought all the materials we needed from the lumber yard and stacked everything in the driveway. My first job, which I was supposed to finish before he got back, was to move all the bricks down to the cellar. I figured I could carry a boxful of six at a time, which meant that I'd have to do more than a hundred trips. I had already done twenty-two.

Right at that moment I didn't think I could lift even a single brick. My arms felt like jelly. My legs didn't feel like anything. I had to look down just to make sure they were still there.

Mom canceled the Tupperware party she was supposed to host that night in the next town over. I told her to go, because she could make ten dollars if people bought a lot of the new colored storage bowls that Mr.

Tupper created. It's hard to believe that women would make a party out of buying plastic storage containers. But these *were* special. After you closed one, you lifted the end a little and it let out a burp, meaning it would seal airtight. When I was younger I used to store my metal army men in one of Mom's old Tupperware bowls. I liked hearing that little burp each time I closed it.

All that night and the next day Mom played games with me, like HiQ and gin rummy and crazy eights, in between doing the laundry and vacuuming and ironing. I had never really watched her before, and I sure was surprised at how much work a house took. I felt guilty asking her to play games, but I did. She let me win every time, even after I told her not to. She said she was playing her hardest, but I could tell she wasn't. Mom just couldn't bear to beat me.

At dinnertime I said I thought I could keep down some chicken broth, and she went to the store to get it. Before she left, she turned on the television for me and worked the rabbit ears to get the picture clear. But as soon as she was out the door, the wavy lines came back, and I had to close my eyes so as not to get dizzy.

A few minutes later a car pulled in the driveway.

It amazed me that she had made it uptown and back so quickly. But when the front screen opened, there was Dad filling the doorway, a large black shadow in the low evening sun. He knew immediately what it meant that I was on the sofa with blankets over me and ginger ale on the table.

"Sick again, partner?"

He made it sound like I was always sick, which wasn't true. I'd had the mumps last year, and the measles the year before, and whooping cough the year before that, which means only one major sickness a year. That wasn't so bad.

"Yeah," I said to him, "Mom says I got the summer flu."

He left his bags in the hallway and came toward me. "The summer flu? There's no such thing." He put his cold hand on my forehead. "Feels normal to me. Your mother's babying you again." He shucked off my blanket so fast that it felt like a blast of wind had whipped over me. "Come on, let's get you up. It will do you good to move around."

I wanted to do what he said, because I knew he wouldn't leave me alone if I didn't. But my legs were stiff, I guess from lying on the couch all day. They wouldn't move.

"Do I have to pick you up?"

I raised myself up on my elbows. "I'm trying," I said, "I really am." I couldn't look at him. I knew the expression on his face and what it meant: How could a weakling like me come from a man like him? I wondered the same thing myself. Suddenly his hands were under my arms, lifting me up and setting me on my feet on the floor. When he let go, I collapsed to the carpet as if my muscles had turned to mush and there was nothing to hold me up. That scared me, because if my legs couldn't hold me up, then what would?

"I don't believe this," he said, turning around and around, which is what he did when he was really angry. "I work hard all week to put food on the table and I have to come back to this?"

Maybe it was because I was lightheaded or feeling weird from inhaling Vicks, but for the first time in my life, I talked back to him. "Then why don't you just leave again? We don't want you here anyway."

He raised his boot and nudged my ribs with its steel tip. "What did you say?"

Gort jumped up from his spot by the sofa and started barking.

"Quiet him down," Dad said, "or I will."

I thought about saying, "Sic 'em," but I figured that would just get Gort kicked out of the house forever. "It's okay, boy," I said. "Jesse *barada nikto*." He kind of snarled toward Dad, then curled back up on the floor.

"Jack!" my mother shouted from the doorway. "What's going on?"

Dad whirled around. "I just came home," he said in his smooth voice, the one he often used with her, "and he said he wanted to try getting up. Then he just fell over." Dad turned back toward me with a smile and wink, as if we really were partners putting a good joke over on Mom. Then he bent down and lifted me back onto the sofa. I felt like a teddy bear in his arms. He said, "I guess you need a little more rest, buddy." It occurred to me then that my father never called me by my real name—*partner*, *buddy*, *him*, anything but Jesse.

Mom dropped her bag of groceries and came rushing to me. She smoothed the covers over my legs, and as she did she searched my face for some sign that Dad was lying. I couldn't imagine what would happen if I said he was. Then she touched my forehead with the back of her hand.

"You're burning up," she said. "Jack, call Dr. Metz right away."

For once, Dad did what he was told.

Chapter 23
THE SNEAKY BELLYBUTTON TEST

When I failed the bellybutton test, the doctor knew it was poliomyelitis, which is the fancy name for plain old polio.

First he sat me up on the couch, with Mom holding me so I didn't fall back. He brought out his rubber mallet and tapped my knees. My legs didn't move. He took a pin and scraped it along the bottom of my bare foot. My eyes told me I should be pulling my foot away, but it didn't move either. He asked me to wiggle my toes. My brain gave them the order, "Wiggle!" They just kind of hung there, off my foot.

Then he pushed up my shirt and checked my breathing with his stethoscope. "That's good, he's breathing normally," Dr. Metz said to Dad, who was standing near the door like he was going to run out when we weren't looking.

The doctor told me to lie down again and then said, "What's that on your bellybutton?" I tried to lift my head to see, and then I just reached down there with my hand. I felt nothing. "Can't raise your head?" he said. It didn't seem to me that I absolutely couldn't, just that I didn't feel like it at the moment.

When he said "polio," Mom looked at him in shock. "It can't be," she said. "I've kept him in all summer. The only place he's gone is church and once to the movies."

"Doesn't surprise me," Dad said. "Polio always finds the weak ones."

"Jack!" Mom said sharply to him.

"I'm just saying the truth, isn't that right, doc?"

"Polio can strike anyone exposed to it," Dr. Metz said, which I figured was telling Dad off. "But it is true that some bodies resist the disease better than others. A lot of people probably have had a mild case of polio and never known it. They thought they had an intestinal bug."

Dad nodded that he'd been proven right and swatted the television set. That was his way of clearing away the static, and strangely enough, it often worked.

It sounded like a Western was on, but Dr. Metz kept leaning over me so I couldn't see. He did all sorts of tests, like poking me with pins and tapping me with his rubber hammer. He went up and down my legs and over my chest and down both arms. Then he rolled me over and did the same thing on the other side. I felt like a piece of steak being softened for dinner. After he was done he said that I had most of the feeling in my arms and chest, but muscle weakness in my legs. "Let's hope the paralysis goes no farther."

He called the hospital in Abington and found it was bursting with polios, most a lot worse off than me, so he couldn't get me admitted before morning.

I didn't want to go to the hospital, not tomorrow or any day. I'd seen in *Life* magazine what happens to polio children in the hospital—they end up in iron lungs.

I wasn't going to let anybody put me in one of them. They were like an iron coffin. My lungs might have been puny, but they were good enough for me. And how would you go to the bathroom in one of them? I didn't want to think about it.

"Don't let him put me in the hospital, Mom, please, I'm fine here. I'm feeling a little better already."

"What can you do for him in the hospital?" Mom asked.

"There's no cure, of course," Dr. Metz said, "but we'll start out with a spinal tap to confirm the diagnosis and then monitor him."

"You already know it's polio, don't you?"

"He has all the symptoms."

"Then he doesn't need to go to a hospital to prove it. Jesse will be more comfortable right here in his own house, where we can take care of him."

Dr. Metz finally agreed that I could stay home for the time being, as long as they tended to me around the clock and I didn't get any worse. If I had breathing problems, they were to rush me to the hospital. Most of all, I had to start stretching exercises as soon as my fever broke.

"I have to be away for work, so don't count on me," Dad said, and it surprised me that he thought we would.

"I'm afraid you can't leave," the doctor said, "for two weeks at least." With that he motioned them into the kitchen, where I wouldn't hear them talking about how bad off I really was.

Chapter 24
QUARANTINED (WHATEVER THAT MEANS)

"Quarantined," Dad said as he brought the tray of chicken broth and crackers up to my bedroom, where he had moved me. "Don't that beat all?"

He seemed to think I should know what the word meant, so I didn't let on that I didn't. I hoped that "quarantined" was something really horrible so that he'd leave. As bad as having polio was, it was ten times worse with Dad there looking at me like it was my fault for being sick.

Mom set up a schedule for looking after me. She sat with me in the mornings and read me the comics and news. On the front page she always went right to the little box headlined "Infantile Paralysis" and told me the number of cases and hospitalizations reported that day in Philadelphia.

"You aren't going to the hospital," she always said. "Don't worry about that."

Dad took his turn in the evenings. He acted like I had some sports injury that would heal soon enough. He said he'd been laid up plenty of times when he was young.

He moved the TV to my bedroom so that I could watch Westerns. He called my favorite cowboy, The Cisco Kid, a sissy, so I called his favorite, Tom Mix, a big dope. Dad said that cowboys were tougher in his day and did their own stunts and that Tom Mix would beat up Cisco in a minute. I said that showed how much he knew because Cisco was a faster draw and would plug Tom Mix with lead in a second. Dad laughed at that, but I didn't see what was so funny. "I guess we'll never find out who's tougher, will we?"

Just before dinner each day, Dr. Metz stopped by to do his poking tests. The most he ever said to me was "You're not getting any worse, that's good news." After about a week he said, "The virus should have done its worst by now. Your temperature is almost normal. It's time you started getting better."

I didn't know how exactly I was supposed to do that, since he wasn't giving me any medicine. All I was doing was lying there in bed. For an hour every day Mom wrapped my legs in an old army blanket soaked in hot water. It was supposed to stimulate my muscles, but all it did was make my skin itch something fierce.

After two weeks Dr. Metz took down the sign he'd put on the front door, which said:

KEEP OUT OF THIS HOUSE!

I'd learned by then that quarantined meant nobody except him was allowed to go in or out for fear of spreading the disease. I bet myself a nickel that Dad would be gone by morning, now that he was free.

Chapter 25
I'M NOT A PRETZEL!

The next day a man came from the local polio clinic. The first thing I noticed about him was his hands—they were huge, even bigger than Dad's. He pulled back my covers, and it was embarrassing lying there in my underpants, especially with Dad looking at me. He thought I was scrawny even with my clothes on.

The man grabbed my right leg and started moving it up and around and down and over. At each point he asked me whether I could feel anything and what could I feel and did it hurt? Of course it hurt. It felt like he was twisting me up into a pretzel. I told him that, and when he kept doing it I cried and yelled. Dad said that my muscles needed to be stretched like this—it was the only way I would get better. I wondered how he knew so much about polio all of a sudden.

The man dropped my right leg and grabbed my

left. "Think of your muscles," he said and tapped my thigh. "Think of this muscle right here moving."

That's what Dad used to tell me when he was teaching me to pitch a baseball. "Think of your arm muscle," he'd say. "Imagine it throwing a perfect strike." It hadn't helped any then, so I didn't see how it was going to now.

The torture lasted an hour. When the man left, he told Dad that it was up to him to do the same exercises on me, no matter if I complained or not. I couldn't believe it—Dad was getting permission to hurt me any time he wanted.

He didn't miss a chance. Three times a day he came stomping into my room, saying, "Ready to roll, soldier?"

I never answered him. Sometimes I pulled the covers over my head, but then he'd jerk them loose at the bottom of the bed and grab my legs.

First he massaged them, which felt pretty good, as much as I could feel anything. Then he did all of the twisting-yanking-pushing motions.

"It's about small improvements," he said, "getting a little bit better one day at a time." He ended the exercises by sitting me up on the side of the bed, propped between two sofa cushions, with my legs dangling into a trash can full of warm salt water. It was a treatment he'd read about in the newspaper. "Might as well try everything," he said.

Chapter 26
GOING NOWHERE

This routine lasted for about a week, and I didn't show much improvement, big or small. Dad decided that the problem was that he was doing the exercises *to* me. The way for me to get better, he said, was for me to exercise myself. He propped me up with pillows on the bed.

"Okay," he said, "try to move."

I could swing my arms okay and swivel my head, but that was it. My legs felt like huge sacks of flour.

"I can't."

"Sure you can," he said. "You're not paralyzed. Dr. Metz says your nerves have just been shocked. And your muscles have gotten weak being in bed so long. It's up to you to get them to work right again."

Up to me? How could that be? If it were up to me, I'd be walking around this minute. I didn't ask for polio, so how could I get rid of it just by wanting to?

I knew I couldn't ask Dad these questions. He'd just start in on one of his war stories. From what he said, you'd think every soldier who fought in World War II had come home with some part of them busted up. He learned to get by with his "bum right arm," as he described it. "A strong mind can overcome a weak body anytime," he always said. Mom never said that, which is why I wanted her to do the exercises with me.

"Your mother's busy," he told me. "She has a lot of other things to do around the house."

I said, "You enjoy torturing me, that's all. You like hurting me."

He looked at me strangely. "How can you say that?"

"'Cause it's true."

"I don't want to hurt you," he said, and for the first time in my life, I could see why Mom believed him so often. Dad had a way of saying things that made you want him to be telling the truth, even when you were pretty sure he wasn't. "I want you to walk again," he said.

Was he blind? "I can't move. My legs don't work. I HAVE POLIO!"

"Do you *want* to be a cripple for the rest of your

life, is that it?" That was such a stupid question, I didn't answer him. "There're places for cripples, you know. Dr. Metz told us about them. The Children's Home for Incurables, the Society for the Ruptured and Crippled. How do they sound? You want to go there?"

"No," I yelled at him, "but I can't help it if my legs don't work. I didn't do anything wrong!"

My eyes were getting wet, and I knew I was going to start bawling any minute. Dad hated it when I cried, so I twisted back on the bed, face down, and wouldn't turn over no matter what he said to me.

Later that day, Mom came into my room with my lunch, and on the tray was a yellow envelope addressed to me. In the corner it said: Charles Atlas, 115 East 23rd St., New York 10, New York.

"You don't usually receive mail," Mom said as she tucked the napkin inside my shirt.

"Not usually," I said.

"You're not getting yourself into paying for something, are you?"

"No, Mom, this is only a booklet. And it's absolutely free."

I waited till she left to open the envelope, and there was Charles Atlas on the cover, in his swimsuit.

"I used to be a 97-pound weakling," the booklet said.

I couldn't believe it. This guy, with the most perfect body of any man on earth, used to be a weakling. A guy even kicked sand in his face at the beach. That's when he figured out how to make himself big and strong.

The booklet described a few exercises that would take only fifteen minutes a day. I was ready to start. I figured I'd exercise thirty minutes or even an hour a day, and then imagine how strong I'd be!

But when I moved the tray off my lap and tried to get out of bed, I remembered—I had polio. Charles Atlas would have to wait.

Chapter 27
THE CASE OF THE MYSTERIOUS VISITOR

You really learn who your friends are when you're stuck home with a disease like polio. Sam and Rudy called on the phone, but I couldn't get out of bed to talk to them. Larry sent over his stack of 3-D View-Master reels, including "Tarzan to the Rescue," where Tarzan jumps a lion who is about to eat Cheetah. Larry gave me a whole set of Tom Corbett reels, too, but they were pretty cheesy. Instead of the real Space Cadet from television, it was just these little plastic guys dressed up in spacesuits.

Some other kids from Cub Scouts sent me comics, including the new *Mad Magazine*, with Alfred E. Neuman on the cover. I think he's the spitting image of Rudy. He looks like this (Alfred, I mean):

Nobody actually came to visit. Mom said she was sure

my friends wanted to see me, but their parents were afraid that my polio was catching. I said the doctor wouldn't have taken down the quarantine sign if it was still catching, and she agreed with me. Still, none of my classmates came.

Except Colette de Lyon. She had the fanciest name in Jenkintown. Last year her family moved down from Canada, the French part around Quebec. She could speak two languages better than I could speak one. But she didn't make you feel bad for not being as smart as she was.

One day I was lying flat in my bed, tossing a baseball over my head and catching it in the glove Dad gave me. At first I counted how many times I could catch the ball straight without dropping it, and I did eighteen twice. Then I decided to see how close to the ceiling I could toss the ball without actually hitting it.

There was a knock on my bedroom door, and I raised myself up as much as I could.

"Jesse?" Mom called in to me.

I figured she was bringing in another exercise man, and I didn't want that. But there was no use pretending I wasn't there. It wasn't like I could jump out of the window and run away.

"Yes?"

The door opened, and of all the people I knew there was Colette de Lyon, wearing a yellow T-shirt with horses on it. She had on dungarees, too, rolled up at her ankles. With her short black hair you'd almost think she was a boy.

"Can't you say hello to your friend, Jesse?"

I'd never thought of her as a friend. She was just one of the girls who sat in the front of the class and raised her hand all the time and answered all the questions. I did notice that she turned around a lot, but I thought it was to look at the stuffed beaver Mrs. Kelly had hanging in the back.

I said, "Hi, Collie."

"Well, I'll leave you two to talk," Mom said.

"Hi, J.J.," Collie said.

J.J.? Nobody had ever called me that before. I squinted up at her.

"Those are your initials, aren't they? I remember from when we wrote our full names on the board. Jesse James MacLean."

"Yeah, those are my initials."

She walked over to my shelves and started picking up things and looking at them. I tried to remember if I had anything weird there that a girl shouldn't see. My mind was going blank. All I could remember was my Mr. Potato Head. He looked like this:

Every few weeks Mom bought me the biggest, oddest-looking potato she could find at the market, and I'd make a new Mr. Potato Head with the plastic nose, ears, and glasses. That seemed awfully stupid now.

"Everybody should have a nickname," Collie said as she passed Mr. Potato Head. She turned toward me, and I saw she was holding my autographed picture of Howdy Doody. Actually, Howdy Doody was a puppet, so he couldn't have signed the picture. I guess Buffalo Bob did it for him.

This was worse than Mr. Potato Head. She'd sure think I was a little kid for having Howdy Doody's picture on my shelf.

"I got that years ago," I said. "I don't watch the show anymore."

"I watch it with my little brother," she said. "He boos every time Phineas T. Bluster comes on." She set the picture back on my shelf and picked up my yo-yo. She spun it down and then tried to pull it back, but the string unwound all the way. The yo-yo was dead in the water. Just like me.

"You have to snap your wrist up," I said. "It's all in the wrist."

Collie nodded. "You can show me how some time, when you get better." She started winding the string back around the yo-yo. "Why did your parents name you Jesse James?"

"Dad thinks we're related to him, like some sixth cousin or something. He likes cowboys."

"He was an outlaw."

"My dad?"

"No, dummy, Jesse James."

"Oh yeah. I think Dad likes it even better that he was an outlaw. Jesse James, I mean."

She put my yo-yo back on the shelf. From the back I couldn't have told her from Rudy, who also had black hair and was the same height.

"Can I ask you something, Collie?"

"Okay."

"How come you dress like a boy?"

She looked down at her clothes. "Girls dress like this. My sister wears slacks all the time, and she's a senior."

I didn't know Collie had a big sister, or a little brother. It seemed I didn't know much about her. I didn't really care that she dressed like a boy. It was easier talking to her that way.

"I brought you something to read," she said.

"What?"

She sat on the side of my bed and reached into her schoolbag, which she carried everywhere. When her hand came out it was holding a bright-yellow magazine—*National Geographic*.

"I'm a member of the society," she said, "so I get these every month. Mom said I could bring the old ones to you."

I read the title—"Nature's Tank, the Turtle."

"I thought you'd like this one first," she said, "since you love turtles so much."

"I never told you that."

She shrugged. "I still know it."

I looked behind her. On the wall was my huge poster of reptiles with giant sea turtles on it. Some of them lived hundreds of years, way longer than people.

There were turtles swimming in the ocean today that had been alive during the Civil War, maybe even before America became America. Turtles probably knew more about the world than a lot of people.

But Collie had never been in my room before, so she couldn't have seen my poster. Maybe she had asked Rudy or Sam about me. It felt weird that she knew what I liked.

"I guess I should go." She walked halfway to the door before turning around. "I just wanted to give you the magazine, since I heard you were sick."

I didn't want her to leave so soon. But I didn't know how to ask her to stay without sounding stupid.

She stopped at the doorway. "Larry said you were all shrunk up from the polio."

"I am not."

"I didn't say it. Larry did."

"Well, Larry doesn't know his head from a hole in the ground. He didn't even come over, so how would he know?"

"He said that's what happens to people with polio, they shrink up and then have to go in an iron lung."

"I'm not shrinking up and I'm not going in any iron lung!"

"I knew he was wrong," she said. "He's kind of a dope."

"A big dope."

"Yeah, a real big dope."

She turned to the door again. "I can bring you more magazines, if you want. Except not the new ones, until after my father reads them."

"I don't care if they're old. They're still new to me."

"Good," she said, "then I'll bring you more *Geographics*."

Chapter 28
WHAT SHE DID, AND WHY I LAUGHED

Collie came every other day or so. Mrs. de Lyon dropped her off on her way to shop, then picked her up on the way home. I asked her why she wasn't afraid to come visit me like everyone else, and she said, "The doctor took down the Keep Out sign. That means you're not contagious."

"How do you know so much about polio?" I said.

"My little brother is a Polio Pioneer. We learned all about it when he got his shot."

The Polio Pioneers were the thousands of kids given a new vaccine against polio earlier this year. Everybody was waiting to hear Dr. Jonas Salk, the famous developer of the vaccine, announce whether it worked or not.

"Your little brother volunteered to get a shot in the arm?"

"My parents promised him an ice cream sundae from Carvel's if he'd do it," Collie said. "My brother would jump off a cliff for an ice cream sundae."

"I wish I'd gotten a vaccination. Then maybe the polio wouldn't have struck me."

"You're too old," Collie said. "They were only giving it to second graders."

"That stinks," I said. "I'm not too old to get polio, so they should have given me the vaccine."

Each time Collie came she stayed a little longer. Instead of running out of things to talk about, we seemed to find more. She always bought me a present from the 5&10, like wax lips or a candy necklace or a pack of baseball cards. She knew to buy the Topps brand that had the thin sheet of bubble gum inside as large as the card. I split the gum in the middle and gave her the choice of which part to take, which Mom said was the proper way to share. Collie always chose the slightly smaller piece.

We played lots of games, like Chinese checkers and Parcheesi. She beat me at first, but then either I got better or she started throwing the games, because

I ended up winning about half the time.

She told me about all the places she'd traveled with her parents, like to Paris and Hawaii and Pittsburgh. I told her everything I'd learned about turtles from *National Geographic*—how they can stay underwater for hours without breathing, how they hibernate for six months under the leaves, and how you shouldn't paint a baby turtle's shell because then it can't grow and the turtle will die or turn out deformed.

She said, "Oh, really? I didn't know that," which made me wonder, why didn't she read the article herself? I guess she wasn't really interested in turtles.

In fact, I didn't know why she was interested in *me*. The only thing I could figure was that she liked me. But why would she like me? Most girls didn't pay any attention to me. Of course, I didn't actually pay attention to any girls, either. Rudy and Dave used to take Becky and Joan bowling after school every Friday afternoon at the T-Bird Lanes, but other than that, nobody in the fifth grade went on dates. At Mr. Moody's Dance School, the boys lined up on one side and the girls on the other for most of the night. When Mr. Moody finally got us together to practice the fox trot, it looked like two robots dancing with their arms sticking straight out. Nobody wanted to get too close.

I was thinking about all of this when I heard some hot rodder laying rubber on the street outside and looked toward the window. The next thing I knew, Collie's lips came zooming at my face. I thought she was going to bite me.

"Hey, what are you doing?" I said, turning away.

"Nothing."

"Nothing?"

"I was going to give you a little kiss, that's all. Do you mind?"

"Sure I mind. Kissing is for girls."

"I *am* a girl. Who else am I supposed to kiss if I don't kiss a boy?"

I thought for a moment. "How about your father?"

"I kiss him every night. It's not the same." She had this green ring on her hand that she was turning around and around, like somebody who's nervous. I didn't see why she would be nervous. She was the one doing the kissing. "Don't you kiss your father?" she said.

Boy was she crazy. "Me kiss Dad?" I shook my

head as hard as I could. "That's like the last thing in the world I'd do."

"Boys kiss their dads. My cousin Pierre kisses his dad all the time—on both cheeks. That's the way they do it in France. He visits every year."

"I never saw anybody kiss on both cheeks," I said.

"Well, they do in Paris. Everybody does, even the men to each other."

I couldn't believe I was talking to a girl about kissing. I never thought when I woke up today that I'd get almost kissed by Colette de Lyon and then talk to her about it for ten minutes. Life sure could be surprising.

"So," she said, "do you mind me kissing you or not?"

"I don't know. I just wasn't expecting it, that's all."

"You mean next time I should tell you first?"

Next time? That meant she was planning on trying to kiss me again. "That would be better," I said.

"Okay," she said, "I'm going to kiss you now. Are you ready?"

"I guess." Her face came at me like a spaceship docking. I saw her lips open a little. Then I felt the kiss. It tickled so much that I broke out laughing. Collie ran for the door so fast I didn't have time to tell her what was so funny. I didn't really know what was so funny.

She came back and grabbed the wax lips she'd given me that day.

"I'm sorry," I said. "I didn't mean to laugh."

"Then why did you?"

"I don't know. It just kind of popped out."

"It was rude."

"I said I'm sorry."

"Okay, then." She sat on my bed again.

"So," I said, "have you kissed other boys like that?"

"You're not supposed to ask."

"Why aren't I?"

"You don't want me to kiss and tell, do you?"

I was about to say yes, but then I thought, no, I sure didn't want her kissing me and telling about it. "You're right. You can't kiss and tell. It's like a sin."

"It's not that bad," she said.

"It's pretty bad," I said. "Bad enough that you never want to do it."

A car horn sounded outside, and Collie stood up. "See ya," she said and hurried out the door.

I looked at the clock on my shelf. She had been

here for an hour and a half. For ninety whole minutes, I had forgotten that I was stuck in bed with this stupid disease called polio.

Chapter 29
THE TORTURE MAN RETURNS

The man with the huge hands came back. The memory of the pain he put me through made me wish I could die and return as a ghost, like on *Topper*. It would be cool floating through the house playing tricks on Dad, like putting bricks in his bag of brushes, or filling his coffee thermos with milk, which he made me drink even though he hated it himself. Sometimes I dreamed I didn't have a body anymore—no muscles or bones or anything else that ached. Ghosts had it good in a lot of ways.

The Torture Man said hello when he came in, but I didn't say hello back. Why should I have to be polite to someone who was going to hurt me? Sure, it was all supposed to be for my own good. But just once I wished that someone would let me decide what was good for me.

After his first visit he left a book about polio for us. Mom read it to me each night before bed. The book said that for years they put polios in casts to keep them from moving, in order to give their sick muscles time to rest and heal. But now there was a new idea: exercise the muscles even if it hurt.

I didn't like the sound of that. I'd suffered through two weeks of contortions from the Torture Man and Dad, and all I got was the hurt, not the help. I still couldn't walk or even stand up on my own. When I had to go to the bathroom, Dad or Mom had to carry me in and sit me on the toilet. That was really embarrassing. It was a good thing I didn't weigh too much, and Mom was pretty strong. Sometimes I couldn't wait for one of them to help me, so they got me an old Tupperware container with a flip top for me to pee into. It was hard getting myself to pee in bed, but when you had to go you had to go, and I was sure glad to have the Tupperware handy.

The Torture Man pulled out a roll of brown wrapping paper and cut off a long piece. Then he pulled back my covers and slid the paper underneath me, from my waist down. With a thick black marker, he traced my legs, from my ankles to just above my knees.

"That's how it's done?" Mom said from the doorway.

"That's how it's done," he said and packed up his things.

How what was done? Why wasn't he going to exercise me? Or had he given up on me? And if he'd given up, then what was he measuring me for?

Gramps used to joke that we should call in the coffin maker to measure him so he'd fit nicely in his pine box. He had a gruesome kind of humor. But I wasn't going to die. Dr. Metz told me that. The worst polio could do to me was . . . an iron lung. They were measuring me for an iron lung!

Mom walked the Torture Man downstairs. I couldn't believe she would do this to me. She'd promised—no iron lung. Besides, I wasn't having trouble breathing. I just couldn't move my legs.

She came back carrying my afternoon tea. I wouldn't drink it. I wouldn't even hold it.

"What's the matter, Jesse?"

"You said you wouldn't let them put me in an iron lung, but you're going to, I know it. That's what he was measuring me for."

She sat on the bed next to me and brushed the hair off my forehead. "He was measuring you for braces, Jesse. Didn't he tell you?"

"He didn't say anything."

"I'm sorry. I thought he explained what he was doing. They're going to make braces for your legs. You'll start out in a wheelchair, and then you'll move on to braces."

"A wheelchair?"

"Yes, Dr. Metz was able to get one cheap from a boy who doesn't need it."

"You mean he got better?"

"I won't lie to you, Jesse. That boy got worse. Now he's in an iron lung. But I know that won't happen to you."

Chapter 30
BOMBS AWAY!

My braces wouldn't be ready for a few weeks. With them on my legs and crutches under my arms, Mom said I'd be able to get myself walking again.

To tell the truth, lying in bed wasn't so bad for me. My legs didn't hurt much anymore, they just felt kind of cold. My neck was still stiff, but I could lift it now and see my bellybutton anytime I wanted to. Polio had done its worst to me, Dr. Metz said when he came next, and left me breathing. I wouldn't need an iron lung. When he said that I asked him again, "Absolutely definitely for sure no iron lung, right?"

"There are no guarantees in life," he said, "but I'm ninety-nine percent sure you won't need an iron lung." I figured that was as close as I could get to being sure.

There were a million things I could do in bed,

like read my comics, draw pictures, listen to the radio. The most fun was putting out my army men. Dad didn't like me playing pretend games, even war, so I had to do it when he wasn't home. Mom got down my box of metal soldiers from the closet, and I positioned them in the folds of the covers, aimed at each other across my chest. I imagined great wars being fought in that bed, and every soldier there, it happened, got an arm or a leg blown off.

One day when she was in the backyard weeding, I made little kamikaze planes out of paper like I'd done outside, then lit them on fire and dive-bombed the enemy hiding under my pillow. The paper burned fast, leaving the scent of sulfur in the air, just like how Dad described his real battle. I closed my eyes and imagined being wounded, my legs mangled, with bombs falling all around me. I had to crawl through marshes and under barbed wire to get back to my buddies. I could hear the bullets whizzing over my head and smell the flames from the exploding bombs. When I opened my eyes, I was amazed to see that I had never left my bed, and it was on fire.

I tried to roll myself to the floor, but my body

was twisted up in the covers. I couldn't kick my legs free. I didn't want to call for help, because how could I explain setting my bed on fire? I grabbed my *Superman* and *Tom Corbett* comics and swatted at the flames. That just made them bigger. My pillow case started smoking. Then the comics caught fire.

"Mom!" I yelled as loud as I could. She didn't answer.

I rolled from side to side, trying to smother the flames with the covers.

"Mom!" I yelled again, and Gort ran into the room, barking his loudest. "Go get help," I said. "Go, Gort, go!"

He took off, barking down the hall. In a few seconds, Dad rushed into my room, still wearing his jacket.

"What's going on?"

"The bed's on fire, the bed's on fire."

He pulled the fiery covers from under me and opened my window and threw them out, along with some of my comics. Then he lifted me up to make sure the mattress wasn't burning, too. When he saw that it was safe, he set me down again. It seemed like he did all of this in only a few seconds.

"So," he said, breathing hard, "what went on here?"

There was never much chance Dad would believe a lie, but I thought I'd give it a try. He sure wouldn't like the truth.

"It must have been spontaneous combustion, which really happens," I said, "'cause we read about it last year in science." Dad didn't say anything. "Spontaneous combustion," I repeated. "That was probably it."

He shook his head at me. "I'll give you another chance. Tell me what really happened."

It was time to come clean. "I guess I was playing war," I admitted, "and I kind of pretended a plane was crashing . . . like that kamikaze guy ramming your ship, remember? Tell me what it was like again, how you got the shrapnel in your arm."

For once Dad didn't take the opportunity to tell his war story. "You foolish boy," he said, and I thought he was going to lay into me for almost burning the house down, but he didn't. "You could have killed yourself if I hadn't just come home."

"Yeah," I said, "I guess I was pretty foolish."

He made me hand over my matches, then searched my nightstand and bookshelf and shoebox in case I had some hidden away. He said there was a lesson I had to learn from the fire, and it was this: I couldn't always count on someone being nearby to save me. I would have to learn to save myself, polio or no polio.

Then he picked me up off the bed and put me down in the middle of the floor.

"What's going on?" Mom said from the hallway. "I was out back and I heard Gort barking."

"Your son lit his bed on fire playing with matches," Dad said. "If I hadn't come home in time the whole house might have burned down, with him in it."

"Jesse," Mom said, "are you all right?"

I had never heard her sound so scared.

"He's fine," Dad said, "but he has to strengthen himself. He can't rely on other people to help him all the time. He hasn't tried moving himself in days."

"Please, don't let him do this to me," I said to Mom, but it was as if there was some invisible barrier across the door that she couldn't get through.

"Your mother's not coming in this room," Dad

said. "If you want her, get yourself over to the door."

"I can't."

"President Roosevelt pulled himself across the floor. You can at least try."

I wiggled myself forward a few inches on my belly.

Dad stepped in front of me. "You're not a snake," he said. "You have strength in your arms. Use them to raise yourself off the floor."

"I hate you, I hate you," I said and pounded his shoe. When he didn't yell at me for this, I figured I could do or say anything. I punched his legs and called him a monster. Nothing seemed to bother him.

"Use me if you want to stand up," he said quietly.

I pulled my way up his pants until I was on my knees. I was amazed that I had gotten this far. He lifted me the rest of the way to my feet. I was standing. It was very strange having my head in the air again. I felt dizzy.

Then he unhooked my hands from his shirt and took a step backward. I had to take a step forward to keep from falling. I couldn't believe it—one leg actually moved. My fingers grabbed for his shirt again. He backed up another step. I knew he wanted me to fall, but I wouldn't give him the satisfaction. I stumbled to the doorway and leaned there, holding myself up. Mom was in the hallway, by the stairs. She was crying.

I turned around to tell Dad off. He was on the other side of the room now, next to my bed. "I did it," I told him. "You thought I'd fall, but I didn't!"

"I knew you could do it," he said. "I'm proud of you."

Proud of me? What was he talking about?

He stretched his hands toward me. "How about walking back to me on your own? I bet you can do it."

Sure I could, I knew that now.

"Come on, kiddo."

I steadied myself against the doorjamb, then started back across the room. I took one step before my legs turned to mush again. I was going to fall. Before I hit the floor, Dad swept me up into his arms and put me back in bed.

Chapter 31
WHEN YOU LEAST EXPECT IT

August 6. The anniversary of the day we dropped the A-bomb on Hiroshima nine years ago. And my birthday. It's weird to celebrate being born on a day when so many people died.

I didn't figure I'd be getting any special present for my twelfth birthday. You don't set your bed on fire and then three days later expect your parents to give you the train set you've been wanting for a whole year. After all, they had to spend money buying me new sheets. And Dad had burned his right hand putting out the flames. That didn't put him in a good mood. It would have been a lot smarter for me to burn my bed *after* my birthday.

It was the first time I'd eaten downstairs with my parents since getting polio. They cleared away my usual chair and pushed my new wheelchair up to the table.

"Happy birthday to you," Mom sang as she brought the cake into the dining room. Dad came in behind her, kind of humming along. Behind him was Gort, yelping like he was singing, too. Whenever there was noise in the house, that old dog was sure to be there making it louder. "Happy birthday dear Jesse," Mom sang, "happy birthday to you."

She set the cake in front of me. I didn't understand what was going on. There was only one candle, not twelve.

"We thought we should cut down on the flames this year," she said, "with what happened . . ."

I felt stupid blowing out one candle. It was like I was a little kid.

"Make a wish," Mom said.

"And don't ask to see my scar again," Dad added.

I thought hard. Two packages sat on the table, neither of them big enough to hold the train set. So there wasn't any point in wishing for that. What I really wanted was for Gramps to take me to New York for my birthday. But wishes couldn't turn somebody from dead to alive, except in the movies.

"That candle's not going to burn all day," Dad said.

Okay, what did I most want in the world? *I wish I could walk again, just like before.* I said this to myself and blew out the candle. Mom clapped.

"It was only one candle, Mom. It's not tough to blow out one candle."

"Nevertheless," she said, "you'll get your wish."

She pushed the two presents over to me. "I'm sorry we couldn't do more," she said, "but money's tight this year."

"That's okay," I said.

It really wasn't okay. I mean, I wanted lots of things from the Hobby Shop, like Matchbox cars and a model airplane. Joey got a stereo for his twelfth birthday, plus a trip to Florida, which is a lot farther away than New York. Money never seemed tight around his house. Why was it always at ours?

The packages were wrapped in the funny papers as usual, because fancy wrapping with dogs or cats on it cost extra. The funnies cost nothing. All you had to do was save the comics section from the Sunday paper. Mom had a drawerful.

I picked up a package the size of a loaf of bread and shook it. Nothing moved inside.

"That's from your grandfather," Mom said.

"Gramps? But he's—"

"He gave it to me the week before he died. He knew he might not make it to your birthday."

I opened the package, and inside was another, smaller box, also wrapped in the funnies. I looked at Mom.

"You know your granddad," she said. "He liked to kid you."

After two more boxes like that, I got down to just about the smallest package you ever saw. There was more tape on it than wrapping. I needed to use a steak knife to cut it open. Inside was a little plastic bag. I opened that and into my hand fell a large coin.

"Oh, my," Mom said and wiped her eyes. "I wondered what happened to that silver dollar. It was his most prized possession."

On one side was a cool-looking eagle, its wings spread. On the other was a woman with a shield saying "Liberty." Underneath was the date—1873.

"That was his birth year," Mom said. "His father gave it to him."

Dad took the coin from me and held it up to the light. "It's in almost mint shape. This is probably worth a lot of money. You could buy a dozen of those train sets you've been talking about if you sold this."

Sold the coin? The idea went through my mind quickly. "No, I'll never sell this. It's from Gramps."

Dad and Mom both nodded. I guess I said the right thing. I put the coin back in the plastic and then in my pocket.

I picked up the second package, which was the size of a shoebox. I felt kind of sick thinking what was inside. Goldberg's, where Mom worked two days a week, sold shoes. The last time I was in there she had me slip my feet into the X-ray machine to measure them to see if I'd grown any. She could get new loafers for me at a discount. That was what was probably in this box. How could I fake being happy at getting new shoes for my birthday?

As I undid the tape on the sides, I looked at the wrapping. It was "Peter Pain," a strip I never read. I turned over the package and saw the ad for the American Flyer train set. This was terrible. Here I was getting something I didn't want wrapped in the paper advertising something I did want.

I peeled off the paper. It was a shoebox from Goldberg's, just like I thought.

"Oh, new loafers," I said, "just what I need."

I didn't need them at all. I couldn't even walk right now, so what did I need shoes for? I sure wouldn't be wearing out my old ones very soon.

I opened the lid of the box. Inside was a bunch of scrunched-up newspaper. I rooted around and felt an envelope. On the outside it said: "Master Jesse MacLean." I opened that and found a letter. It said: "Thank you for your recent order of the American Flyer Electric Train Set. We are pleased to ship you the sixty-seven-piece Elevated Trestle Train Set in one week. We are sure you will have many hours of enjoyment with your American Flyer."

I couldn't believe it. I looked at Dad, then Mom.

"It's what you wanted, isn't it?" she said.

I hadn't ever wanted anything as much, except for a dog, and I already had Gort. "It's perfect," I said. "I can set it up in my room as soon as it comes, right?"

"Sure you can," Mom said. "It's wonderful to see you excited again."

She leaned over, and I gave her a hug. I glanced

at Dad. He was rubbing his arm where the scar was. I guess it was hurting him again.

"It was your father's idea to get you this," Mom said. "He sent away for it."

He leaned over my wheelchair. I reached up and put my arms around his neck. He smelled like Burma-Shave.

"Thanks, Dad," I said.

I felt him give me a little kiss on my face. I thought about kissing him back, but before I could decide to, he pulled away.

It seemed strange to me. All the times I had wished to get the train set, I hadn't. This time I didn't wish for it, and I was getting it. I was sure that meant something, but I didn't know what.

Chapter 32
THE GIFT THAT CHANGED EVERYTHING

The next day Collie came over with a bag from the 5&10. I imagined all the candy that might be inside—Necco wafers, Sugar Daddies, wax bottles, Atomic Fire Balls. Eating a Fire Ball was like biting into a hot marshmallow—you knew it was going to burn, but you still did it. Rudy would put three Fire Balls in his mouth at once. He could have been a fire-eater in the circus.

Collie handed me the bag, and I opened it. Inside was a large white pad with thick sheets and several pens with very sharp points. No candy.

"What's this for?" I said, trying not to sound disappointed. I'd really been looking forward to something sweet.

"It's a birthday present."

"You didn't have to get me a present."

"I wanted to. I figured drawing was something you could do with all your time in bed."

I opened the pad and ran my hand over the paper. It was the thickest I'd ever seen. "How do you know I draw?"

"You draw on your book covers at school all the time."

"That's just doodling," I said. "It helps me concentrate when the teachers are talking."

"I think it's art."

"Art? Like hangs on walls? You're crazy."

"There's all kinds of art," she said. "Like . . ." She looked around my room and spotted my stack of comic books. She picked up the top one, *Nancy and Sluggo*.

"Like this," she said, waving it in front of me.

"*Nancy and Sluggo* is art?"

"Maybe it's not real art, but people get paid to draw comics, you know. I bet you could do it."

Sure I could draw. I had a stack of pictures I'd done just since summer started. And I was getting better at drawing people, too. But comics?

"What would I draw comics about?"

She shrugged. "You could create a superhero."

"They've all been invented already, like Captain America, the Human Torch, Black Cobra."

"That's only three."

"Okay, there's Spiderman, Superman, Rocketman, Dollman, Plastic Man . . ."

"You give up too easily."

"That's what my dad says."

She sat at the bottom of my bed.

"They're all super *men*," Collie said. "You could do something different."

"Like what?"

"Like about something you know."

I thought for a minute. Nothing came to mind. Could it be that I knew nothing special about anything?

"Turtles," Collie said. "You know about them."

"Yeah, turtles. You're right. I probably know more about them than any kid I know. But what could a turtle do?"

"Maybe it could be a mutant turtle that's super fast and it can stand up on its legs and give karate chops to people. Then whenever it's in trouble it just sinks into its superhard shell that even bombs can't crack open."

Collie was usually pretty smart, but this was about the silliest idea I'd ever heard. "Nah," I said, "nobody's going to believe a super mutant karate turtle."

"I guess you're right." She stared at me. "There must be something else you know."

I braced my arms on the bed and pushed myself up so I was sitting higher. There was something I knew a lot about from Gramps: *baseball*. "I can recite the whole Phillies starting lineup," I said. "Richie Ashburn, center field; Granny Hamner, second base . . ."

"There's a baseball player named Granny?"

I had never thought about it before. Granny was a pretty weird name for any guy, let alone a ball player.

"Yeah," I said, "and there's Smoky Burgess, he's the catcher, and—"

"I got it!" Collie said.

"Got what?"

She smiled at me. I thought she was teasing.

"Come on, tell me."

"Polio."

You know how sometimes at Christmas your mom hands you the last package from under the tree and you get all excited because it has to be something special? Then you open it and see three Fruit of the Looms or a couple pair of argyles. You feel like you've been rabbit-punched in the stomach.

"Polio?" I said. "Nobody wants to read about a stupid disease. That's boring."

"No, see, your superhero could have polio, like you do, but it gives him special powers."

"Polio takes away your powers, Collie."

"Listen, when somebody goes blind, sometimes he gets better at other things, like hearing. My uncle Don's blind, and he can tell when people come in the room, even if they're trying to sneak up on him. He says he feels them. So maybe you get special extra power because you have polio."

What she was saying sounded great, but like Dad always said, where's the evidence?

"I haven't exactly noticed any special powers, Collie."

"We're not talking about you," she said. "We're talking about the kid with polio in your comics."

"Okay, so what special power could the super-hero polio kid get?"

"Maybe he could read people's minds."

"Nobody can do that."

"That's the point, dummy, it's a *special* power. You could call him The Polio Kid."

"Who's going to read a comic called *The Polio Kid*?"

She frowned at me, which made her look kind of like Mom. "Look, I'm doing all the thinking here. You come up with a better name."

At the bottom of my bed was the booklet about New York, The Wonder City. If there was a superhero boy who saved people in The Wonder City, he would have to be called . . . "The Wonder Kid!"

Collie smiled and nodded. "Perfect."

Chapter 33
WHY IN THE WORLD DO THEY MAKE GREEN JUJYFRUITS?

In the next few days I learned that it's a lot easier to come up with a great idea than it is to actually carry it out. Like Mom says, Easier said than done.

First I had to decide on The Wonder Kid's special power. I didn't think reading minds was interesting enough, and besides, how do you draw a guy reading someone's mind? So I tried out other possibilities. I had always liked the idea of being invisible so that you could sneak into the movies without paying. The Invisible Wonder Kid would look like this:

Then I thought about a kid who could hear everything, even from miles away. But so what? Who ever wished they could hear better, except for old people like Gramps who couldn't hear much at all?

I thought that maybe the kid could make opposites happen, but that got tricky. For instance, if The Wonder Kid wanted to stop a person falling out of a window from hitting the ground, then the opposite would be to make the person fly up in the air, which wouldn't be good either, if you think about it. If he wanted to stop a person from burning in a house, then the opposite would be to flood the house with water, which could drown someone. You had to be very careful about the special powers you wished for.

"Not going well?" Mom said as she came into my room. That was pretty obvious from the pile of crumpled-up papers on the floor. Every time I messed up a drawing, I balled it up and threw it in the air toward Gort. He barked and batted at it for a while, then sat there waiting for the next one.

"I can't figure out my superhero polio kid's special power."

She picked up the papers and straightened other things in the room. Wherever Mom was—in my room, the kitchen, the living room—she was always straightening something or putting it in its proper place. And while she was doing that she'd hum or sing something. But she never knew all the words to tunes, so she just kept repeating phrases, such as *sh-boom, sh-boom*, which is from the new song "Sh-Boom."

She picked up Mr. Potato Head, fixed his ears on straight, then turned to me. "If your hero has polio, then his super power should have something to do with the disease."

"Like what?"

"Well, polio makes it hard for people to walk, so maybe your superkid can run really fast. You could call him The Blur because nobody could see him when he was running, so he would have a secret identity, like Superman and Batman."

Mom put Mr. Potato Head back in his place and then started singing "Sh-boom, sh-boom" as she walked out of my room.

Collie liked the idea of The Wonder Kid being a super-fast runner. "We could make him be twice as fast as Roger Bannister," she said.

"*You* know who he is?"

"Sure, it was in all the papers when he broke the four-minute mile. Don't you read *The Bulletin*?"

"We get the *Inquirer*."

"Everybody reads *The Bulletin*."

We were sitting on my front porch, sipping lemonade. It took a lot of effort to get there. First Mom carried me from my bed to the stop of the stairs. Then I kind of slid down on my backside, one step at a time, with her lifting my feet so they didn't catch on the rug. At the bottom she picked me up again and took me outside.

She said the fresh air and sun would do me good. I *was* looking awfully white for July. Usually by this time my skin would turn brown from being outside playing wiffle ball all day at the playground. If I didn't get a tan soon, guys would start calling me Casper, like the friendly ghost.

"What good is it for him to run superfast?" I said.

"He could get away from danger that way."

"Superheroes run *to* the danger, Collie. When they run away from it they're yellow."

She slurped the last drop of lemonade from her glass.

"Okay, so maybe The Wonder Kid doesn't move fast himself, but he's able to make other things move just by thinking about them. Like he could move a person out of the way of a train that's coming toward them, or he could move a boulder in front of a bank door to keep robbers stuck inside."

I liked this idea. The kid who couldn't move much at all could make other things move however he wanted. That was a super power that would come in very handy.

When you solve one problem, you often find yourself facing another one. Ours was this: How did The Wonder Kid get his power? You couldn't have him wake up one day and be able to move things around just by thinking.

"Pez?" Collie said and flipped one up for me. "It's lemon," she said. "Do you like lemon?"

"Sure," I said, "I eat any flavor." That was true with Pez but not with some other candy, like Jujyfruits. I hated the green Jujyfruits. When you pulled out a piece in the movie theater, you couldn't tell in the dark whether it was one of the terrible-tasting greens, or a black licorice, which was okay. If you put it in your mouth and tasted the green, then you had to take it out and stick it under the seat. The bottom of every seat in the Hiway was probably covered with green Jujyfruits.

Collie popped a lemon Pez for herself. "You get a high fever with polio, don't you?"

"Yes."

"Okay, so maybe the fever boils The Wonder Kid's brain and puts him in a coma and he almost dies. When he wakes up he has the power to move things to save people from bad things happening to them."

"A fever can do that?"

"In the comics," Collie said, "anything can do anything."

Chapter 34
ME AND THE JDs

What should have been the worst summer of my life was turning into a pretty good one, and that was because I had a best friend to share everything with. I know it sounds weird—my best friend was a girl. I wouldn't have believed it myself a couple months before. If you'd asked me which will happen first, a man will walk on the moon or you'll have a best friend who's a girl, I'd have bet on the man on the moon.

Collie and I didn't have much in common. I had never traveled anywhere interesting like her, and I'd never ridden a horse like her. She couldn't yo-yo like me, she didn't know anything about model trains, and she never watched cowboy shows. The strangest thing of all was what she did seem to like—me! And me with polio. I couldn't explain it. Dad said it was strange, too.

So I asked Collie one time, "How come you like me?"

"Well, you're pretty smart, for a boy," she said. "And you're . . ."

"What?"

"You're cute."

Me, cute? Imagine that.

But just when you think things are going great, something happens to upset the apple cart, which is how Gramps used to put it. It was the afternoon Collie pushed me uptown to Stutz's for an ice cream cone. This was my first trip out in the wheelchair beyond our street. I could roll myself along the sidewalk if it was flat, but I couldn't make it up hills or over cracked pavement, and there was a lot of that between my house and Stutz's. I needed to be pushed. It was embarrassing being wheeled around by a girl, but I didn't have any choice. Dad was off selling brushes. Mom had housework. Nobody else was volunteering to do it, and I was itching to get out of the house.

No place in the world smelled better than Stutz's. It was like walking into a candy factory. The air was filled with chocolates and mint bark and macaroons and nuts all mixed with the flavors of ice cream in big vats under the glass. Mom said she put on five pounds just going through the door. I could have spent all day there.

You could smell Stutz's half a block away since they made their own candy. I was awful excited about going inside. But when Collie turned my wheelchair around the corner at Greenwood Avenue, we came face to face with the thing I kept forgetting about: steps. There were three stone ones leading up to the door of Stutz's.

"Rats," I said, "steps."

"I'll go in," Collie said. "What kind do you want?"

"Chocolate, two scoops, in a sugar cone."

I gave her a dollar, which would be more than enough. It was my whole allowance for the week.

"You okay waiting here?"

"Sure," I said, "why wouldn't I be?"

As soon as Collie went inside, I found out why I wouldn't be. Three kids came walking across the street from the firehouse: the Dean brothers and Marty Scaggs, who always hung out with them. I knew this meant trouble. They were the kind of juvenile delinquents you read about in the magazines. If there was a rumble happening, they were leading it. If you heard cars screeching in the middle of the night, it was probably one of the Deans. They were JDs, and they seemed proud of it.

"Hey kid," Scaggs said, "that your girlfriend pushing you around?"

"She's not my girlfriend."

"Then what is she, your babysitter?"

I wished I could reach out and slug him so hard he'd cough up his guts, but that was hard to do from a wheelchair. I wondered what The Wonder Kid would do in this situation. The three of them were standing right next to the fire hydrant, so I concentrated with all my might to make the top pop off and have the water soak them. That would make them run.

Nothing happened. All I had for weapons were words, and I remembered some that worked in the comics. "Beat it, lame brain, or I'll decompose you."

The Dean brothers laughed and pointed at Scaggs.

He stepped closer. He looked a lot bigger than when I could stand up. "What did you say?"

"It's just a line from a comic book," I stuttered out. "I didn't say it, the kid in the comic did."

Scaggs lifted one side of my wheelchair so that I was almost falling out.

"Take it back or I'll dump you."

"Let him go," said Tommy, the older Dean brother. "You can't beat up a cripple."

Was that some sort of rule that even the JDs followed? I didn't plan on being a cripple forever. But as long as I was, it was nice to know that.

"Who says you can't?" Scaggs said and tipped my wheelchair forward until I rolled out onto the sidewalk. It happened so fast that I could barely get my hands out to break my fall on the pavement. But that didn't hurt as much as seeing Scaggs laughing over me. He was close enough to kick, and I would have—I really would have—but my legs wouldn't move.

"You *are* a lame brain," Tommy said. I thought he was speaking to me, but when I looked up, he was standing face to face with Scaggs. "What are you going to do next, knock over old ladies?"

He shoved Scaggs back and then bent over to me. "You okay?" he said.

"Yeah, I just skinned my hands is all."

He waved to his brother, and together they lifted under my arms and set me back in the wheelchair. "Sorry about Marty," Tommy said. "He gets stupid sometimes."

"I do not," Scaggs said.

"Shut up," Tommy said, "before I knock *you* over." He looked back at me. "Polio?"

I nodded.

"My cousin got it last year. He's walking again now. You'll walk, too, if you try hard enough."

"I will. My dad does all of these exercises with me. I know I'm going to walk again."

He punched me lightly on the arm. "Okay, kid, see you around." With that they were gone.

"Sorry I took so long," Collie said as she came out of Stutz's carrying two large ice cream cones. "What did those boys want?" She nodded at the three of them walking up the street.

"Nothing," I said, licking the curl of chocolate on top. "We were just talking baseball."

Chapter 35
COMICS BY . . . J. J. MACLEAN

At home in bed that afternoon, I drew three comic strips. The first one was about a kid in a wheelchair being pushed to the starting line of a race. All the runners laugh at him. But when the gun goes off, he turns into The Wonder Kid with a rocket on his wheelchair. It shoots down the track like a blur.

In the second strip, a bully bumps into a boy on crutches in the theater, sending his popcorn flying. Then the boy becomes The Wonder Kid and imagines the bully being sucked into the popcorn machine.

In the third strip, I pictured a polio kid standing—well, not really *standing*, you know what I mean—up to Marty Scaggs. I drew Stutz's, I drew a juvenile delinquent who looked a lot like Scaggs starting to tip over the kid's wheelchair, and then the final drawing: The Wonder Kid using his mind to open the fire hydrant and spray Marty.

I wasn't going to show these drawings to anyone except Collie. I felt embarrassed even doing that. But she had given me the pad and pens. Besides, I knew I couldn't hide anything from her.

She liked the hydrant one the most. She said it showed I had a very good imagination, which was funny because I was only remembering what happened to me in front of Stutz's. I didn't have to imagine anything except the ending.

Then Mom came in to hang up some shirts she'd ironed, and Collie said, "Here, Mrs. MacLean, take a look at what Jesse drew."

"I'm not really finished," I said quickly and tried to grab them from Collie's hand, but she was too far away.

"Your mother's allowed to see," Collie said. "You should be proud."

Mom read the first one, smiled a little, then looked at the second and laughed a little. By the third comic she was smiling and laughing. "These are very good, Jesse," she said, "as good as *Beetle Bailey*. You should be in the newspaper."

"That's what I think," Collie said. "My father

knows the editor at the *Times Chronicle*. He could take your comics in and see if they'll run them."

"I'm just a kid," I said. "They won't want my comics."

"How do you know unless you try?" Collie said.

"There's no harm in trying," Mom added.

They were ganging up on me. Collie slid my drawings into her school bag. I didn't have a choice. That's the way it goes when you're lying on your back in bed—you don't have a say about a lot of things.

Chapter 36
MY GOOD NEWS

The *Chronicle* is going to run *The Wonder Kid*!

Collie called to tell me the news. The phone in the hall wouldn't reach into my room, so Mom stood in my doorway repeating Collie's message. What she said was: "They're going to publish your comics, and they want you to do one every week."

I felt like jumping up and down, but all I could do was sit up and pound my mattress.

"I'm going to go get your father so you can tell him the news."

"No, Mom," I said, "maybe later. You know Dad doesn't like to be bothered when he's working downstairs."

"Your father has been fooling with that fallout shelter all day," she said. "You'd think the Russians were going to drop the bomb on us tomorrow."

She left to call him and I thought, *Maybe the Russians are planning to bomb us tomorrow.* How would we know? It wasn't like they'd send us a letter beforehand. They'd drop an H-bomb on us and then we'd drop one on them and they'd bomb us again and we'd bomb them. Pretty soon the whole world would be blown to smithereens. It could give you nightmares thinking about what could happen in a nuclear war. But at least I wouldn't have polio anymore—that was one good thing about being hit by an H-bomb.

I heard Mom pulling Dad down the hall.

"What's so important that it couldn't wait?" he said as he came in my room. His hands were red, like he'd been working with bricks. I sure wished I could be down there with him.

"Jesse had some good news today," Mom said. "Tell your father."

"Well," I said, and I really wished she hadn't dragged him all the way up from the basement. With him staring at me, I felt like my news wasn't important at all.

"Come on, out with it," he said. "I've got mortar hardening."

"Well, the *Times Chronicle* is going to run my comic strip in the paper every week."

"And pay him," Mom added.

"Pay him? How much?"

"Five dollars a week."

"Well, that's nice," he said. "We'll be living with a big shot now, earning five dollars a week. I suppose you'll be spending it on movies and candy and such."

"No, Dad, I—"

"Darn right you won't. Nobody gets to waste money in this house. It's about time you started saving for your college."

"Oh, Jack," Mom said, "let him enjoy his money for a few weeks. He's been having a rough summer."

"A lot of people have it rough, a lot rougher than lying in bed all day."

The way Dad said this, he made it sound like I was choosing to lie in bed with polio. That made me mad.

"It's my money," I said. "I can spend it on whatever I want."

"Then I guess you won't need any allowance from us anymore. And maybe you should start paying for all the food you eat."

"Stop it, Jack. He's not paying for his food, and he's not giving up his allowance. Whatever he earns we'll put half away, and he gets to spend the other half however he wants, no questions asked."

"Is that so?"

"Yes, that's so."

With that, Mom left the room, meaning the discussion was over. For once she'd gotten the last word.

"So," Dad said, "with all of this drawing you're doing, you've neglected doing the leg exercises I showed you, haven't you?"

"A little, I guess."

"You want to lie in bed all your life drawing comics, or do you want to walk again?"

Of course I wanted to walk again—that's what I wished for on my birthday cake—but I also wanted to draw comics. "Can't I do both, walk and draw?"

Dad picked up the stack of comic books from my desk.

"This is the kind of crazy stuff you want to make, *The Vault of Horror*, *The Haunt of Fear*?"

"It's not crazy, it's funny."

"Comics rot your brain. They're ruining kids

today. I should take all these away from you."

"No, Dad, you can't do that."

"I *can't* do it?"

"I mean don't do it, please."

He put the comics back on my shelf. "If you're not going to do your exercises on your own, I'll have to do them with you."

I couldn't believe it. He meant now.

"What about your mortar? It'll harden, won't it?"

"You let me worry about the mortar. I'm going to wash up and give your legs a workout."

The way he said it, I knew I was in for torture.

Chapter 37
SPENDING MY MONEY
(I THINK I GOT GYPPED)

When the editor of the *Chronicle* paid me for my first comic strip, I couldn't stop staring at the money. Abe Lincoln wasn't the best-looking president ever, but his face sure looked good to me on the five-dollar bill.

This was the first money that I had earned from a real job. I didn't want to fold the bill to go in my wallet, so I held it on my lap while Collie pushed my wheelchair out of the newspaper building and onto the sidewalk on Johnson Street.

"What are you going to do with your money?" she said.

"My mom says I have to save half of it."

"That leaves two dollars and fifty cents."

"I was thinking of buying—" Wait a minute. Should I really be telling Collie I was going to send away for the complete Charles Atlas exercise program for kids so that I wouldn't be an eighty-four-pound weakling anymore? She might laugh at the picture of Mr. Atlas in his swimsuit. She might tell the other kids.

"You were thinking what?"

"Well, now that I have the train set, I need a town to go with it."

"A town?"

"Yeah, they sell buildings like houses and schools and stuff that you place around your train tracks to make it look like a real town. It costs $29.95. But you can put one dollar down and then pay two dollars every month. That's what I'm probably going to do."

"Oh, I see. That sounds like a very good deal."

Collie didn't seem very happy to hear how I might spend my money. She pushed me across West Avenue, but then instead of going on down Leedom toward home, she steered me along the sidewalk on West. I waved to Mr. Dewine, the shoe repair man, who always left his door open, even in winter. Mom sent me up there with her shoes to get the heels fixed. Mr. Dewine wore a long smock that had black and brown smudges all over it. He smelled like shoe polish.

Some older boys came out of Carter's Drugstore laughing and shoving each other. I looked away, so I didn't know if they saw me or not. I was hoping they didn't see me. Sometimes it's better to be invisible to people, but that's hard to do in a wheelchair.

At the corner Collie turned me down York and stopped my wheelchair so that I was staring into the 5&10. The sign in the window said: BANANA SPLITS, 1 CENT. At the bottom, in much smaller letters, it said, PICK A BALLOON AND PAY THE AMOUNT SHOWN INSIDE, FROM 1 TO 89 CENTS.

Collie bent over to tie her shoe, leaving me to stare at the sign. An idea occurred to me. "I know what I want to do with part of my money."

"What?" she said, standing up.

"Buy us banana splits."

"Oh," she said, "I don't think I could eat a whole banana split myself."

"Then we'll get one and share. Come on, maybe it will only cost me a penny."

A man coming out of the 5&10 held the door open so Collie could push me in. It was a tight squeeze to move my wheelchair down the aisle to the lunch counter. Several people coming toward us had to flatten themselves as we passed.

Then came the real problem. Sitting in the wheelchair I couldn't see over the soda counter. I felt like I was only three feet tall again. There was no way to get onto a stool. Collie wasn't strong enough to lift me, and I wouldn't have let her anyway.

"Can't park there," a man behind us said. "You're blocking the aisle." I tried to turn around to see him, but I couldn't twist my head far enough. For all I knew it was Mr. 5&10 himself.

"We better go," I said to Collie.

"No," she said and flipped the brake onto the wheels with her foot so I couldn't move. "We want to buy a banana split," she said to the man.

"You have to sit at the counter to eat. That's the rule. Your friend will have to wait outside."

"He wants a banana split, too," she said, "and he's paying."

"Look, children."

"We're not children!" Collie said in the loudest voice I ever heard from her. She pointed at me. "This here is the famous artist who draws the comic strip called *The Wonder Kid*. It's in all the papers."

"Is it now? That's great, I'm sure, but I still need to keep this aisle free for customers."

"*We're* customers," Collie said, "and you can't make us leave."

Everybody sitting at the counter turned toward us. I thought I recognized some of them from church. I sure didn't want it to get back to Mom that Collie and I had made a scene on my second day out.

"I think he *can* make us go," I whispered to Collie. "It's his store."

"My father's a lawyer," she said out loud. "They can't make us leave if we want to buy something and have the money. Show him your money, Jesse."

I held up the beautiful new five-dollar bill.

"The young lady has a point," the man at the end of the counter said. He leaned into the aisle, and I saw that it was B.J., eating his hot dog covered with relish, like he did every day at noon. Everybody knew B.J., but not what his initials stood for. He spent all day walking around the ball fields and down to the train station and uptown to the stores and he would have walked downtown, too, except we didn't have one in

Jenkintown. Some people called him the mayor of Division Street, which is where most of the colored lived, because he always wore a jacket and tie and spoke to everyone he passed. It was like he was a politician running for office, making friends with everybody.

B.J. wiped his lips and stood up. "Why don't you push the wheelchair over at the end here, and then the young lady can have my seat?"

"You sure, B.J.?" the manager said. "You haven't finished your hot dog."

"There'll be another one tomorrow. These young folks are in desperate need of a banana split."

"Thank you very much," Collie said as she pushed me into the space at the end of the counter.

B.J. tipped his hat to her. "And whom do I have the pleasure of talking to?"

"You have the pleasure of talking to Colette de Lyon."

"Mademoiselle," B.J. said and bowed halfway. Then he looked at me. "You're Jack MacLean's boy, aren't you?"

"Yes."

"I could tell. You've got the look of him at his age."

"I do? Everybody says I look like my mom."

"Maybe on the outside, but I see inside people, and there you're the spitting image of your father."

I didn't know exactly how B.J. could see inside people. I guess he had a special power. I wondered if he could tell what people were thinking, too.

"I haven't seen your father around town," B.J. said. "What's he doing now?"

"Dad, well, he's a salesman, so he travels a lot."

"I'm sure he's good at that, Jesse. He's overcome a great deal in his life." B.J. put two dollars on the counter. That seemed like an awful lot to me for eating only half a hot dog. I guess he was a big tipper. "You two make an awful fine-looking couple," he said, "awful fine."

I felt my face burning red, but Collie didn't seem embarrassed at all. "Thank you," she said and held out her hand for B.J. to shake. "Glad to make your acquaintance."

Chapter 38
LEARNING HOW TO TIP

Here's how it worked with banana splits at the 5&10: Different colored balloons hung on a string behind the counter. When you ordered a split, you got to pick a balloon and pay whatever amount was written on the paper inside. Kids always tried to lean over the counter and see into the balloons. That never worked because the paper inside was folded over. The 5&10 had thought of everything.

"Which color do you want?" Collie asked.

I scanned the row of blue and green and yellow and red balloons. I closed my eyes and it came to me. "Yellow," I said. "Pick the yellow."

"We'll take yellow," Collie said.

"All righty," the woman behind the counter said, "yellow it is." She took a long pin from her hair and popped the balloon, which made everyone look over. Then she unfolded the little paper and held it over the counter for me to see. "Eighty-eight cents."

"One cent off? That's a gyp," I said.

The woman shrugged. "I don't fill the balloons, sonny, I just pop them."

"I bet there aren't any one-cents in the balloons," Collie said.

"My friend Rudy got fifty cents once, but everybody else I've seen has been either eighty-nine or eighty-eight."

"I'm going to tell my father," Collie said. "He'll make them pop all the balloons to prove there's a one cent in there."

"Then he'll be eating a lot of banana splits," the woman said.

I pushed myself up as far as I could on the arm rails of the wheelchair, but I still couldn't see over the counter, which was very annoying. I loved watching a banana split being made almost as I much as I enjoyed eating it.

"What's she doing?" I asked Collie.

"She's scooping out the ice cream. Vanilla,

chocolate . . . and there goes the strawberry."

You could get all of one flavor if you wanted, but I liked the mixture—Neapolitan, it's called.

"Now she's grinding nuts over it."

"Ask for extra," I said.

"Could we have extra nuts, please?" Collie asked. Then she turned to me. "She's giving us extra nuts."

"A lot or a little whipped cream?" the woman said.

Collie and I looked at each other. "A lot," we said at the same time.

"It's almost done," Collie said. "She's getting out the cherry."

Nothing in the world tastes like a bright-red maraschino cherry. I ate half a bottle of them one time. Later that night I threw up every last one, which made for the reddest vomit you ever saw. At first I thought I was throwing up blood, which really scared me. Mom said I had just learned the definition of sickeningly sweet.

It isn't easy sharing a banana split when you're sitting in a wheelchair and your friend is up on a stool. We decided that we'd each take two spoonfuls, then pass the dish to the other. Collie said I should go first since I was paying. I said she should go first since she was the girl. For a few moments the banana split sat on the counter with neither of us eating it.

"It's going to melt pretty soon," I said.

"It's already started."

"I know," I said. "You sit on the footrest under the counter, then we'll be at the same level and we can eat at the same time from opposite ends."

And that's what we did.

When we finished, the woman took away our dish and brought the check. "That will be eighty-eight cents," she said. I handed over my beautiful five dollar bill. She took it without realizing the special occasion. This was the first thing in my whole life that I had ever bought with money that I had earned.

"My father framed the first dollar he made," Collie said. "It's hanging in his office."

"Too late for that," I said.

The woman brought back my change and laid it on the counter. I reached up and brushed it into my hands—four dollar bills, a dime, and two pennies. Then I started to panic. I knew I was supposed to tip, but how much? The only place I ever ate out with Mom and Dad was at the automat in Willow Grove where you picked your own food from behind little glass doors. There was nobody to tip. B.J. had left two dollars for a hot dog that only cost sixty-nine cents, so it seemed that I should leave at least a dollar.

I reached up and put the bill on the counter.

"What's this?" the woman said.

"It's a tip."

"A dollar tip? I appreciate the thought, young man, but a dime would do just fine."

I put the dime on the counter and took back my dollar. That made me feel better. I still had $4.02 left, and $1.52 of it was for me to spend however I liked. I was full up with half a banana split and had money to spare in my pocket. Plus, I was hanging out with a girl who had kissed me. What could be better?

Chapter 39
WATCH OUT, BURMA-SHAVE!

"Jesse," Mom said, coming in my bedroom door, "I have a visitor for you."

"Wait. Pull up the blanket."

"Are you cold?"

"No, it's . . . the sheets."

"Your bucking bronco sheets?"

"Shhh, Mom."

"I thought you liked the new cowboy sheets I bought you," she said as she drew the blanket over me.

"I do, but I don't want Collie to see them."

"It's not Collie who's here today, Jesse."

Mom leaned into the hall and motioned to someone. A tall man in a suit came into my room. "Hello there, Jesse," he said as he walked toward me with his hand out.

Dad told me it was important to shake hands

hard to make a good impression. But when I put my hand out, the man grabbed it and shook it, then let go. I didn't do anything.

"My name's Mr. Fitch from the National Foundation for Infantile Paralysis Office in New York, Jesse."

"The what?"

"You probably know us as the March of Dimes."

"Oh, yeah, that's the group President Roosevelt started to help polio kids. I sent in five dimes last year."

"Did you, now?"

"It was half his allowance for the week," Mom said as she picked up my dirty T-shirts from the floor.

"That was very generous of you. If more people gave like that, we'd lick this disease." The man looked around my room the way Collie had when she first visited. "I saw your comic strip in the *Times Chronicle*."

"You read the *Chronicle* in New York?"

"Not normally, no. Someone in our Pennsylvania office sent it to me and said I should take a look at the work of a certain boy who has polio."

"Who's that?"

He laughed. "Why you, of course. You draw *The Wonder Boy,* don't you?"

"Yes."

"I think it's wonderful, if you don't mind the pun."

"What's a pun?"

"You know, 'The Wonder Boy' being *wonder*ful."

"Oh, yeah, I get it."

"And you draw this all by yourself? Nobody helps you?"

"My friend Collie, she helps me think up ideas sometimes. Then I draw them."

"That's fine. At the March of Dimes we're always looking for interesting children for our ads so that people can see the real face of polio. How would you like to be on a poster?"

"Like the ones on the highway?"

"Well, you'd be the poster child for this region, so your picture might be on a few local billboards or in the newspapers. What do you think?"

I didn't know what I thought. My picture on a billboard like a Burma-Shave ad? That was weird. I leaned to the side to see around the man. Mom was standing there with her arms folded.

"I think it would be exciting," she said. "Not every boy gets picked for something like this. It's an honor."

"What would I have to do?"

"We'll have a photographer come out and take some pictures of you in bed, in your wheelchair, maybe drawing. That's about it, except some reporters might want to ask you questions later. You don't mind talking about your polio, do you?"

I shrugged. "Guess not."

"Good, you'll do fine. I'll work out the details with your mother." He leaned over my bed. "Mind if I see what you're working on?"

I turned my pad around to him. It was a drawing of a kid in a wheelchair at the 5&10. He wants a banana split, but he can't see over the counter. So he uses his special power to shrink everything, except himself and his friend.

"Very clever," the March of Dimes man said, "a disabled boy with super powers. This happen to you?"

"Sort of," I said, "except I couldn't shrink everything."

"Yes, that would be difficult. Well, I'll leave you to your work."

He put his hand out again, and this time I managed to give a good hard shake.

"Anyone ever tell you you look a little like that boy on *Rin Tin Tin*?"

"Rusty? No, 'cause he has freckles and curly hair."

"Yes, but except for that, you look just like him, the all-American boy."

Chapter 40
SMILING WITH POLIO

The photographer from the March of Dimes came the next day. He took pictures of me in bed doing my drawings. He took pictures of me sitting in my wheelchair wearing my Hopalong Cassidy hat. He took one picture of me hugging Gort. When the flashbulb popped, that old dog dashed out of the room.

I had never smiled so much in my life, and I didn't like it. My face was starting to hurt. Besides, what kid smiles when he has polio? It seemed to me I should be looking real mad, but the photographer said people didn't give money to help angry kids. They gave it to help nice kids.

So I smiled and looked nice.

A week later, the poster arrived, wrapped in brown paper. I wanted to open it right away, but Mom said

Dad was coming home that night, and we should wait for him.

"Why?" I said.

"Because this is a family event, and he should be included."

"He's almost never around for family events."

"That's because he's away working for us, Jesse. When he is here, we include him in everything."

So we waited for Dad. He looked awfully tired when he came home just before dinner. He barely said a word. He drank two beers and went out back to smoke a couple of times. He said he'd had a bad week on the road. I guess that meant he didn't sell many brushes.

"Maybe we should wait on showing him the poster," I said.

"Nonsense," Mom said. "It will cheer him up."

So when Dad came inside and asked what was for dinner, Mom said, "Baked ham, your favorite. But first, Jesse has something to show you."

"What is it?"

She pulled out the rolled-up poster from the closet and set it across my lap.

"It's just a little thing," I said as I slid off the rubber band. "We waited till you got home to open it."

"Looks pretty big to me."

I slipped out the poster. There I was, Jesse MacLean, sitting in my wheelchair with my pad in my lap, as if I were drawing. Across the top, in giant letters, it said: YOU CAN HELP!

Dad stared at the poster like he didn't know what it was.

"It's for the March of Dimes," Mom said. "Jesse is going to be the March of Dimes poster child for this region next year."

Dad's face turned the deepest red I ever saw. I knew right off that he was angry, but I wasn't sure about what.

"When did this happen?" he asked.

"While you were gone a man came from the March of Dimes to interview Jesse. They thought he would make the perfect poster child because of the comic strip he does, and the way he looks. They said he's the all-American boy."

"An all-American boy with polio."

"Sure, that's the point. That's why they wanted him."

Dad took the poster out of my hand and looked

at it closer. "You think you look good in this picture, boy?"

I didn't know what answer he wanted. It seemed like I might get in trouble answering either way. "I guess I look okay," I said, trying to find some middle ground.

"You proud of this picture?"

"Proud? No, I mean, it's just a picture they wanted to take. I don't know if I'm proud or not."

"You should be ashamed."

"Jack," Mom said, "why are you saying that?"

"You think it's a good idea to advertise to the world that our son's a cripple?"

"It's not an ad, Jack. It's a poster to get people to give money to a good cause."

"Why don't we just hang a sign on the house, 'Here lives a cripple'? Is that what you want," he said to me, "everybody thinking of you as the poor little polio kid?"

"No, Dad."

"Then why did you do this?" he said in his angry voice. "Why?" he shouted. "Why?"

"I don't know I don't know I don't know," I said. Then I covered my ears so that I wouldn't have to hear anything else he said. I should have covered my eyes. Dad took the poster in his hands and ripped it straight down the middle. It felt like he was ripping me apart, and I didn't have any way to stop him.

Chapter 41
THE SURPRISE PICTURE

My braces arrived. They had thick leather straps that wrapped around my knees and metal rods that ran down the sides of my legs to keep them straight. With crutches in my hands, I could stagger a little ways stiff-legged, kind of like Frankenstein's monster. I felt as if I might topple over any second.

Once you learn how to ride a bike, you always know how. I figured it was the same with walking. But now I had to practice swinging my left leg out along with my right crutch, and then my right leg with the left crutch. Walking had never taken any thought before.

Dad moved the coffee table and lamps out of the way in the living room for me to practice. "It's just like watching you take your first baby steps," he said. "You were scared of falling then, too. But when you fell you got right up and tried again. In a week you were running around the house like a holy terror."

He was remembering something nice from when I was two years old. But I wasn't fooled. I knew what he was really thinking.

"You just want me to get better so you won't have a polio kid for a son," I said. "That's why you tore up the poster of me. You're embarrassed that I'm yours."

He looked surprised that I said this, which surprised me.

"No, buddy, that's not it. I just don't want you to get hurt in this world."

What was he talking about? "I'm already hurt!" I said as I made it across the room for the fifth time and flopped onto the sofa. I unhooked the stupid braces and tossed them away.

I figured he was going to yell at me, but I didn't care.

"Okay," he said, "if you want to walk like a cripple all of your life, that's up to you."

I practiced on my own when he was gone. It wasn't easy keeping my balance. And my arms ached from holding myself up with the crutches. But the more I did it, the stronger I got. I even started to feel my legs a little. Best of all, I could move on my own again. Nobody needed to carry me to the bathroom. No more peeing into Tupperware.

One place I'd been wanting to go back to was Gramps's room. Mom said she had left everything like it was, except for cleaning up the mess from the night he died.

I hobbled down the hall and stood in front of his room. I started to say, "Hey, Pancho, it's me," like usual, then just nudged open the door. I almost expected him to be there, sitting up in his bed, listening to the Phillies on the radio.

His room was quiet. His bed was empty. I moved in and looked around. I went over to his bureau and picked up his metal coin box. I shook it and heard the rattling of his Indian head pennies inside. I wondered whom he had left those to. I wished it was me.

Next to the coin box was a piece of red plastic, what Gramps used to call his "rose-colored glasses." He said, "Hold this in front of your eyes and the whole world looks a lot better." I raised the plastic over my eyes, and everything turned a soupy kind of red. It was interesting seeing this way, but it wasn't any kind of magic red plastic. It didn't bring people back from the dead.

I picked up a package wrapped in brown paper, tied with a string. This was the family Bible, passed down through generations. I had never been curious to open it when Gramps was alive, but now I undid the knot. Inside was the fattest book I ever saw. It must have been six inches thick. When I lifted it from the wrapping, little pieces of leather came off the cover. That didn't stop me. I remembered what Gramps said: "It's good if a book is falling apart. Means people are reading it."

I opened to the first page, and there was a sheet of paper marked "August 6, 1942," my birth day. Underneath was a four-leaf clover, faded brown, and the words: "Welcome to the world, Jesse James. May luck be with you forever."

I traced my finger around the four-leaf clover. It was the first one I'd ever seen. I'd spent whole afternoons last summer looking in our yard and never found one. I was hoping it would bring me luck in the Duncan yo-yo competition uptown. I did my doggy bite and shoot the moon and loop the loop perfectly, but I still couldn't beat this kid named Cheetah who was a wizard at yo-yo.

You'd have to have a whole pocketful of four-leaf clovers to face him, and even then you'd probably lose.

I turned more pages to a part of the book bulging a little. I opened up and saw a bunch of old pictures. There was Gramps behind the wheel of a cool-looking roadster; and Gramps riding a horse; and Gramps on skis, just like he said, ready to go down the ravine. He hadn't been lying to me. He *had* lived a whole interesting life before I was born.

I held up the next picture, which was of a boy on the beach. His hair was all wet, as if he'd just come in from a swim. This picture seemed newer than the others. It couldn't be Gramps. I turned the picture over and saw "John, 12." That made me laugh, because this John kid was the same age as me and even skinnier. I slipped the picture back in the Bible and—

I looked at it again. John was Dad's real name. Jack was just his nickname. This had to be him. He had told me all about growing up near the ocean. What he didn't tell me was that he'd been a runt of a kid, just like me.

I heard heavy footsteps in the hall. I slipped the picture into my shirt pocket and turned around as Dad pushed in the door.

"Didn't you hear me calling?"

"Ah, no, sorry."

"What are you doing in here?"

"Nothing," I said, standing in front of the Bible. "I was just looking at things. Gramps let me look at anything I wanted when he was . . . you know."

Dad stared at me a moment without saying anything. It was like he was trying to pierce into my brain and figure out what I was really doing that I wasn't telling him. I wanted to hold up his picture and say, "How can you call *me* puny? Look at how you were!"

What I said was, "Time for dinner?"

Chapter 42
SHAKE, RATTLE, AND ROLL

Each morning now I'd get up, go the bathroom to wash my face, pull on clothes, and then slide down the steps on my rear end. I held my crutches over my head like they were rifles I had to keep dry while wading across a river. I often found it easier to do something if I imagined myself a soldier. After breakfast Mom would find some project for me to do in the kitchen or on the front porch. Every day I practiced walking.

When Collie came over in the afternoon, we played checkers in the living room. Gort sat on the floor watching. Sometimes when I reached to make a move, he'd bark like I shouldn't do it. Usually he was right— I'd walk right into some trap I didn't see and get double-jumped. I don't really think that dog knew how to play checkers, but he sure seemed to.

One day Collie had just kinged herself again

when the room grew suddenly dark, like a giant black curtain had been pulled over the windows.

"Looks like a thunderstorm," I said.

"Not a thunderstorm," Mom said as she came in the living room, "a hurricane."

"Really?"

"That's what the radio says. Hurricane Carol's going to hit us tonight. Your mother just called, Collie. She's picking you up in a few minutes. You collect your things while I go batten down the hatches."

Batten down the hatches? I didn't have any idea what that meant. "Where are you going, Mom?"

"To make sure things are put away outside. I don't want our trash cans and yard chairs flying down the street at ninety miles per hour."

"A hurricane," I said to Collie when Mom left, "it's the most powerful force on earth. I've read about them, but I never was in one, were you?"

She shook her head. "I don't want to be, either."

"Why? They're exciting."

"Hurricanes kill people, you know."

That's exactly what made them exciting—a tree could fall on you or the wind could blow out your windows or the little creek that ran by the train tracks could turn into a raging river. A hurricane turned things dangerous that normally weren't any problem at all. That seemed exciting to me.

Hurricane Carol started with a little rattle of the downspout outside the living room window. A half hour later the wind was whistling through all sorts of small openings in the house I never knew were there. Then the rains came. It was like God was emptying barrels of it from the sky. The water gushed down our street as if it were a river. After just an hour it overflowed the drainpipes and was creeping up the front lawn.

"What if the water keeps rising?" I said as I watched from the front window. "It could come into our house. Maybe we should put sandbags around the door."

"The water won't reach that far," Mom said, but she didn't sound very sure of herself. Dad always sounded sure.

She pushed aside the curtain and watched the rain pelting the street outside. "I wish your father would get home. I'd feel a lot better."

After a minute I hobbled to the kitchen and

looked out the back window. The giant willows were swaying back and forth as if they were dancing. Our neighbor, Mrs. Klecko, had left some of Mr. Klecko's shirts pinned on her clothesline. They were flapping in the wind like flags. I bet those shirts would be miles away by the end of the hurricane.

The lights flickered off for a moment, then came back on.

"Candles," Mom said as she opened the cabinet over the refrigerator. "We may lose power." She got down three thick ones. "Take these to the living room, Jesse, while I look for more."

I limped over to the counter, clicking at every step. Why did braces have to make that *snap-snap* sound? It was bad enough having polio. You didn't need to call attention to it. If scientists could invent an H-bomb, why not silent braces? That would be a good invention.

"I'm sorry, Jesse," Mom said, "I forgot you can't carry things."

I didn't like her thinking that. I wasn't a cripple. "Yes I can, Mom."

I stuck one candle in my shirt pocket and the

other two in my pants pockets. It was a tight squeeze. Then I got my crutches and wobbled into the living room.

A burst of wind suddenly whipped against the house, and I fell over onto the sofa just as if it had blown me down.

A minute later Mom came in with an armful of candles. "That last blast knocked out the phone line," she said. "Your father can't even call us now. He'll probably wait out the storm wherever he is, instead of driving in this."

For the first time I could remember, I wished Dad *would* come home. I didn't like to admit this, but I was scared. I had always thought it would be exciting, swirling around in a tornado or a hurricane. Instead it was just plain scary.

The lights flickered again, then went off. The house became black as, well, how I imagined the inside of a coffin, like where Gramps was.

Mom struck a match and lit two candles. A different light filled the room. It was soft and orange, not bright white like regular light.

"This is how people lived for thousands of

years," Mom said, "with just candles for light."

I couldn't imagine being without electricity. That meant no TV and no lights. "What did they do after dark?"

"The adults sewed clothes or fixed tools. The children read and—"

A clap of sound like a hundred bullet shots made us twist our heads around.

"What was that?"

"I don't know," Mom said. "I'll go see."

She took a candle and hurried to the kitchen, leaving me alone. It was spooky with the rain pounding on the roof and the wind rapping against the windows. The hurricane had our house surrounded.

I heard the back door open. I couldn't tell if Mom did it or the wind had burst through on its own. A rush of wet warm air came whooshing down the hall.

"Mom?" I called out.

She didn't answer. I grabbed my crutches and slipped my hands into the holders. I couldn't walk and carry a lit candle, so I just aimed toward the kitchen and took off into the dark. I brushed past the sofa and into the dining room. That was a dangerous place, with the table on one side and the china cabinet on the other. If I hit that, I'd surely break the glass and Mom's best china.

I inched along as carefully as I could. I remembered making fun of how slowly Gramps walked down the hallway. Well, a worm would have beaten me now, too.

I made it to the kitchen doorway and called out again, "Mom?" I heard nothing but the wind whipping through the back door. Where could she have gone? It was as if the storm had lifted her off her feet, just as in *The Wizard of Oz*.

Chapter 43
"MOVE, LEGS, MOVE!"

The world outside the house was as dark as inside. This was the way it was for blind people all the time, I thought. How did they keep from being scared?

I pushed open the screen door and yelled out the back, "Mom! Where are you?" Giant raindrops banged on the tin roof of the garage, making an awful racket. The wind was so strong it was like sticking your face in front of a huge fan turned up high. I couldn't even hear my own words.

I didn't know what to do. Why couldn't Dad walk in now, like he had when I set my bed on fire? How come Gort wasn't right next to me to help, like Rin Tin Tin, instead of upstairs hiding under my bed? I was on my own.

I hadn't tried going down steps with my braces yet, but it seemed that's what I had to do—and in a hurricane! I stuck one crutch out and one leg, then the other crutch and the other leg. I got down the three steps and moved out from under the eaves. The rain soaked my skin in a second. I was as wet as after diving into a lake. I turned the corner where our house jutted into the yard and got hit with a gust of wind so fierce it punched me to the ground.

Now I was wet and muddy and couldn't see or hear a thing except wind and rain. I felt like just lying there, letting the hurricane sweep me up and set me down again in some other world where kids didn't get polio.

Then I thought of Dad in the war, having to jump into the Pacific when his ship was blown up. Here I was just getting wet in my own backyard. If he could float for an hour in the ocean with his bad arm to save himself, I could certainly get myself back inside the house. Mom was probably in there now, wondering where *I* was.

I felt around for my crutches. They weren't there. That made me really worried. How could I walk without them?

I reached out my hands in all directions, but I

could feel nothing but mud. I had to try moving without them. I was always good at rolling races in the grass, so I did that, rolled over twice and ran smack into . . .

What was it, a big tree limb? The rain was stinging my eyes so that I could barely open them to see. I wiped my face and squinted. Mom! She was just lying there, and I didn't know why.

"Wake up, Mom, wake up." I shook her shoulders. I tugged at her arm. She didn't move. I leaned over her and put my cheek close to her mouth. I held very still, and after a few seconds I could feel her breath. She was alive.

I had to get help, fast. I rolled to the house and pulled myself up along the wall. I figured I could find my way back to the door this way.

But then what? Mom said the phone was out. I couldn't call for help. It was no use going inside.

I turned around and started the other way, toward the Kleckos'. The rain was coming down sideways now, straight into my face.

"Move, legs, move!" I ordered them, as if I was The Wonder Kid with special powers. They didn't start running or anything. There wasn't any miracle. But my legs were holding me up, even without the crutches, and that was good enough. I leaned against the wall and used my hands to lift each leg forward, one step at a time.

I don't know how long it took me to get to the back of our neighbors' house. Their place was connected to ours, so it should have taken only a few seconds, but it seemed like minutes. I sat down on their steps, then raised myself backward until I could reach the door. I pounded on it, praying that there was someone inside to hear me.

In a minute Mrs. Klecko opened up and said, "My Lord, Jesse MacLean, what are you doing out playing on a night like this?"

Chapter 44
SAVING MOM

I'm not sure all that happened next. I know they dragged me inside their kitchen, which was lit up by candles. Then they came at me with towels. I had to shove them away and yell, "My mom, she fell in our yard. She's hurt."

"Well, why didn't you say so?" Mrs. Klecko said.

Mr. Klecko put on his raincoat and went out with a flashlight. I wanted to go, too, but I knew that was stupid. I had done all I could. Mrs. Klecko pulled off my wet shirt and tried to yank down my shorts. I squirmed until she stopped. Then she took a towel and rubbed my head so hard I thought my ears were going to fall off.

Pretty soon Mr. Klecko came in the back door with Mom. She was standing up now, but she looked all groggy, like she would fall over if he let go. He put her in a chair at the kitchen table, and Mrs. Klecko opened a bottle of smelling salts under her nose. Mom twisted her head to get away from the awful smell, and then her eyes opened.

She saw me sitting in the chair across from her. "Jesse, are you all right?"

"He's fine," Mrs. Klecko said, "just a bit wet. It's you we're worried about."

Mom rubbed the back of her head. "Something hit me," she said. "I stepped outside, and something hit me from behind."

"Probably a tree limb," Mr. Klecko said. "You shouldn't go outside in a hurricane, you know."

"Yes," Mom said, "you're right."

Chapter 45
ME, JESSE!

The lights and phone came back on the next day, just before Dad pulled into our driveway in the Buick. Mom and I met him in the hallway.

"Boy, was that an adventure last night," he said as he came through the door and dropped his case of samples. "You wouldn't believe what it was like being out in that hurricane."

"Wouldn't we, Jesse?" Mom said and gave me a wink.

"We have no idea," I said.

Dad knew something was up. "Okay, what's going on? What happened?"

"Nothing much," Mom said, "except your son walked without his crutches in the middle of the storm to rescue me."

Dad looked at me with his "You've got to be kidding" expression.

"He rescued you? From where?"

"I went out back to check on a loud bang during the storm and got hit in the head by a flying branch. It knocked me out for a few minutes. I might have been lying there for hours if Jesse hadn't come find me. A tree could have fallen on me."

Dad reached out and felt Mom's head. "Are you all right?"

"I'm fine," she said, moving his hand to where the bump was. "Just a little sore. Jesse went for help next door."

Dad turned to me. "You went outside on your own?"

"Yes sir," I said.

"At the height of the wind and rain," Mom added.

He rubbed above his lip, where he had a little mustache growing. "You might have fallen yourself," he said, "then you both would have been stuck out there."

"I guess so," I said, wondering what he was getting at.

"You remember I taught you how to do SOS in an emergency?"

"Sure, three quick raps, three long raps, then three more quick raps." I was proud that I remembered.

"I told you that's the signal I worked out with Mr. Klecko next door. All you needed to do was tap out SOS on the wall, and he'd come help. You have to use your head in an emergency."

I couldn't believe this. He was complaining that I hadn't rescued Mom the right way—his way! It was amazing how quickly things turned from good to bad with Dad around. I couldn't even look at him, especially with that stupid mustache starting under his nose. It made him look like a different man, but he was acting like the same old lousy father.

"It doesn't matter what I do," I said, staring at the hall floor. "You always say I'm wrong."

"When you do something right, I tell you."

"No, you don't, you always tell me I'm wrong and puny."

"I never told you you were puny."

"You told Mom. I heard you."

There, I got him. He couldn't deny he'd called me puny to her. That would be a lie.

"Well," he said, "I'm sorry you heard that."

Dad apologizing? I didn't think I'd ever heard him do that before.

"But you are small for your age," he added, "that's a fact."

I felt inside my shirt pocket. The picture was still there, and now was the time to use it. "How about this fact?" I pulled the old photo of him out and held it up. "You were scrawnier than me."

He snapped the picture out of my hands. "Where'd you get this? I threw it away years ago."

"And I saved it years ago," Mom said, "in the family Bible. It's time you stopped running away from the past, Jack. Jesse is old enough to know things."

Dad walked into the living room, but it wasn't as if he were running away. It seemed like we were supposed to follow him, so I hobbled in and sat on the sofa. Mom sat in the easy chair. I guess we were having another family conference.

"Okay," he said, standing over me, "you old enough to hear the truth?"

I nodded, but I didn't know what truth was coming. Was I adopted? Was I really the milkman's kid? Whatever the truth was, I just hoped it wasn't about me.

"You're right, I was scrawnier than you," Dad said. "I had spinal meningitis when I was ten, and I had to stay in the hospital for a year before they cured me. I got teased all the time about being small. I only made the football team because the coach needed bodies to sit on the bench. In the navy I wasn't any hero, I was a cook. When I got out, the only thing I was fit to do was sell brushes." He took a deep breath. "There you have it, the whole sorry history of your father."

I didn't understand. Dad teased for being small? He never played football? He was a cook in the navy? This didn't make sense. He always acted like he was great at everything.

I had all sorts of questions, but they came down to this: "But then why do you always yell at me for not being able to do stuff?"

"Because I found out the hard way that you have to be strong in this world."

"Like Charles Atlas?"

"He's strong physically. You have to be strong mentally, too. That's what I try to teach you. You're a lot smarter than me—you get that from your mother. You can be anything you want. You don't have to settle for selling brushes."

"That's not so bad," I said.

Dad laughed like he knew I was kidding. "Every time I walk up to a door, somebody calls out, 'The Fuller Brush man's here.' I'm not a name or a person to them. I'm just the man who sells brushes."

It was odd hearing Dad talk like this. I thought he liked his job. At least I hadn't heard him complain. I never knew you could hate doing something and not complain about it. I couldn't imagine waking up each morning to a job I hated. It would be like having to take the trash out all day, every day.

"Why do you think I drive to other towns to sell brushes?"

He wanted to get away from me, that's what I thought.

"It's because I don't want people in Jenkintown thinking of me as the Fuller Brush man," he said. "I sell to strangers. That way I don't embarrass the family."

"We're not embarrassed about your job," Mom said. "You make a good living."

Dad looked at Mom. "I don't think everybody in this room agrees with you." He turned back on me.

"You are embarrassed to have a father selling brushes, aren't you?"

How did he know that? When kids asked me what my dad did, I'd just say he was a salesman. If they asked what he sold, I'd say, "You know, lots of different things." Before they could ask another question, I'd say, "What *does* your dad do?" I should have said, "My dad sells brushes, like the kind everybody uses in their house. It's a pretty interesting job because he gets to travel around and meet all sorts of people." Why couldn't I tell them that?

It was strange. When Dad was away I wished something bad would happen to him so he'd never come back. Now that I was facing him, I couldn't bear hurting him with the truth. But if I said I wasn't embarrassed, he'd know I was lying. I seemed to always get myself into these jams where I had two bad choices. I never seemed to get two good choices.

I decided not to answer his question at all. "I like you better this way," I said.

"Which way—being a failure all my life?"

Was that it? Was I glad that he was a failure because then I could be one, too?

"No, I just like it better knowing you weren't some super kid when you were young, that you were kind of like me."

"Kind of like you," he said and rubbed his mustache again. "I guess you're right, Jesse. Maybe we're more alike than we know."

Jesse—it was odd hearing him say my name. For the first time it actually felt like he was talking to me, not some other kid he wished he had.

I didn't even think about it, I just reached up my arms to him. When he leaned down, I kissed him on the cheek. Before he pulled away, I kissed him on the other side, too.

"Two kisses?" Dad said.

"That's how the French do it, on both cheeks."

"Even the men?" Dad said.

I nodded. "Even the men."

Chapter 46
INSIDE THE FALLOUT SHELTER

I've heard people say that the truth hurts. I guess that's true if you tell some girl she's ugly or some boy that he's a moron when they really are. Either one might punch you.

But the truth about Dad didn't seem to hurt anybody. It did seem to change him. He didn't let up on my exercises, though. But instead of yelling at me to do them, he started giving me rewards, like candy or extra TV time. The best reward was that he promised to take me for a tour of the fallout shelter when I could cross the living room without my crutches. That happened three days after the hurricane. In the middle of the room I had to reach out to the chair to steady myself, which was really cheating, but Dad said I'd come close enough. He would take me down to the cellar.

Gort came with us. I told him he had to be on his best behavior, and when I said, "Sit, Gort," he surprised me by actually squatting in the corner of the shelter, just inside the door. Dad patted him on the head.

Even though I hate small places, I loved the fallout shelter. It wasn't really much smaller than my bedroom. It felt safe in there, like a great hideaway.

It smelled of bricks and paint. There were shelves all around the walls, stacked with soups and tuna fish and canned vegetables and boxes of cereal. There was a cot on one side and a rolled-up sleeping bag on the other. That was for me.

I plopped down on the cot, and a great idea came to me. "This could be my room, Dad. I could make all the noise I wanted down here and not bother you and Mom."

"There are laws against kids sleeping in cellars," he said as he checked the ceiling. I guess he was making sure it could stand a bomb blast.

"You mean they can tell you where you can sleep in your own house?"

"Yep, the government can tell you how to do a lot of things."

"Can I at least play here sometimes?"

"It's not a playhouse. I don't want anything messed up."

That meant the only time I'd ever get to be in here was if we actually were attacked. I didn't wish the Russians would send over an H-bomb, of course, but at least then I'd get to use the shelter. I figured that was looking for the good in a bad situation, like Gramps told me to do.

"What would we do all day in here, Dad?"

"A lot of reading," he said, "that's for sure. Your mother's in charge of choosing books for us. And then there's this." He reached under the cot and pulled out a box. Inside was Monopoly, Parcheesi, Clue.

"But you don't like playing games," I said.

"I don't like doing a lot of things. That doesn't mean I won't do them. And look here."

My eyes followed his finger to the wall.

"I bored a hole through to run in an electrical cord. If we have enough notice of a bomb coming, we can move the TV down and watch Westerns."

"You think they'll be running Westerns during a nuclear war?"

"Never know, *pardner.*"

I liked the way he said it this time, as if we were two cowboys holed up in a cave. Like Gramps and his radio, Dad was going to be prepared just in case things turned out better than expected.

Chapter 47
MY LAST DRAWING

September 1. The calendar says that summer will last three more weeks. But calendars are for adults. Kids know that summer ends as soon as school starts, and for me that was the next day.

Collie came over this morning, and her mother drove us to station park for one last afternoon out. Gort barked so loudly when I started out the door that we let him come with us.

I didn't take my crutches, but I still had to wear my braces, and that clicking sound made everybody look, as always. When we walked through the tunnel under the tracks to get to the creek, that *snap-snap* sound echoed off the walls. Some older kids on bikes passed us and started pointing and laughing at me. But when Gort snarled at them, they beat it fast. He looked up at me as if saying, "Please, just this once can't I go bite them?"

I would have liked to say, "Get 'em, boy." But I figured I couldn't have Gort bite every kid who made fun of me. There were a lot of places he couldn't go with me, like to school and into stores. I'd just have to get strong, like Dad and Charles Atlas.

"Jesse *barada nikto*," I whispered into Gort's ear as I held his collar. He stopped snarling, but he didn't look happy about it.

"Why are boys always so mean?" Collie said as we came out on the other side of the tracks.

"I'm not mean," I said.

"You're right," she said and slipped her hand in mine. "You're different."

Mom told me I had to give up doing my comics for the *Chronicle* and concentrate on my schoolwork now. I said I could concentrate on schoolwork and comics, but she said no, that school was too important.

She let me draw one last strip. In it a kid with polio and his family are in their backyard. An H-bomb goes off over the city, and the blast blows everybody to the ground. His mom and dad are knocked unconscious. But the boy turns into The Wonder Kid, who, with his trusty Wonder Dog, drags his parents into the fallout shelter in the cellar. In the last frame they sit playing cards, with The Wonder Dog curled up on a chair. The strip looked like this:

Dad looked at my drawing and said that this Wonder Kid was quite a boy.

AFTERWORD

Church bells rang out across the country on April 12, 1955, as if to celebrate the end of a war. In fact, Americans were rejoicing at the news that a powerful enemy—polio—was soon to be defeated.

On this day, people sat by their radios to hear the results of a year-long trial to inoculate children against the paralyzing disease. They were not disappointed. Dr. Jonas Salk reported that the new vaccine he developed was both safe and effective, sparking cheering in the streets.

Polio was on the minds of every parent and child in the 1950s. In 1952, the disease sickened 57,628 in the United States, paralyzing about 21,000 of them. In 1954, the year Jesse MacLean catches polio in *The Wonder Kid*, another 37,741 were stricken.

The disease most often hit children, and it did so primarily during the hot summer months. Nobody knew at the time how polio was transmitted. From a water fountain at a school or theater? From getting overheated? From swimming in a pool? From touching someone infected? Parents didn't take any chances. They kept their children at home as much as possible during the long vacation from school. Scout troops were disbanded, playgrounds and pools deserted, and sports canceled. Instead of being a time of fun for children, summer meant fear.

Doctors now believe that polio is passed between people through water or food contaminated by feces carrying the virus. An infected child who does not wash his hands after going to the bathroom might transmit the virus in a handshake, for example. Sharing a sandwich or soda could mean sharing the virus, too.

While thousands of children came down with serious symptoms during the early 1950s, most of those exposed to polio suffered only flu-like symptoms, or no symptoms at all. In the worst cases, though, the virus attacked the nerves that control breathing. These unfortunate children were rushed to hospitals and put into iron lungs to keep them alive.

An iron lung is a metal cylinder slightly larger than a human body. The victim, often a young boy or girl, was put into the iron lung from the neck down. When air was pumped out of the machine, the child's lungs rose, which allowed air to flow in through his mouth and nose. When air was pumped back into the machine, the lungs fell, forcing the air back out through the nose and mouth. In this way, iron lungs enabled polio patients to breathe.

Nurses could tend to the children by reaching through small openings in the side. Sometimes sufferers regained the ability to breathe on their own in a few weeks. In other cases, they had to remain in these machines for many years, lying on their backs, with just their heads visible to the world.

Less severe cases, like Jesse's in this story, could be cared for at home. In a treatment devised by an Australian nurse named Sister Elizabeth Kenny, children were put through strenuous daily exercises to keep their muscles active. It felt like torture to them.

Dr. Salk created his vaccine by killing live poliovirus with heat and the chemical formaldehyde. He believed that when injected into a person, this killed virus would stimulate the body's immune system, which fights all disease, to produce antibodies against it. These antibodies would stay in the bloodstream for years, perhaps for life, ready to fight the poliovirus whenever it attacked.

Before he could test his vaccine on a large number of people, he had to demonstrate that it wouldn't actually give them polio. In 1953, he proved his theory by vaccinating himself, his wife, their three children, and more than a hundred other friends and colleagues. No one came down with polio. The vaccine seemed safe.

Salk next had to show that his vaccine would work on a large group. During 1954, 650,000 second-graders volunteered to be injected. These children became known as the Polio Pioneers. Some received the Salk vaccine while others received what's called a place-bo—a simple sugar solution that isn't the real vaccine. Neither the children nor their doctors knew which of the Polio Pioneers had received the Salk vaccine and which had received the placebo. (Scientists often do their experiments like this so the results can be judged objectively.) Another 1 million children did not receive the vaccine but were monitored to see how many got polio. It was the largest medical experiment ever.

The results were dramatic: the vaccine cut polio rates in half. Based on this news, children across the country were vaccinated. By 1962, the number of polio cases dropped to just 1,000. But there were problems: the vaccine wasn't 100 percent successful, and it had to be given by injection.

Another doctor, Albert Sabin, developed a different vaccine that included just enough live poliovirus to provoke a response from the immune system, but not enough to actually cause the disease. Most important to children, his vaccine could be given by mouth in a sugar cube. They liked that much better than a shot in the arm.

A carving on an Egyptian stone from about 3,500 years ago pictures a boy with a shrunken leg, the telltale sign of polio. This evidence leads scientists to conclude that the disease has been around for centuries. Why, then, weren't more cases reported in the past?

The answer may be that for most of human history, people were exposed to polio in the unsanitary conditions around them. The virus didn't make infants terribly sick in part because they still retained immunity to the disease, passed on from their mothers at birth. Because of this early exposure, these children developed their own antibodies, which protected them for a lifetime.

During the 1900s, many countries improved their water and sewer systems, reducing various microbes. With better sanitation, children often were not exposed to the poliovirus until they were eight or nine years old. By then, their bodies had lost their natural defenses against it. When polio hit them, it could strike hard. Sometimes being "too clean" can actually lead to worse disease.

The most famous person to be stricken with polio was Franklin Delano Roosevelt, president of the United States from 1933 to 1945. He came down with the disease when he was thirty-nine, before he was elected. He could not walk or stand up without someone supporting him. Still, many Americans didn't realize he had polio. That's because only two pictures were ever taken of him in a wheelchair, and neither appeared in a newspaper before he died. Today a statue of Roosevelt, in his wheelchair, sits near the National Mall in Washington, D.C.

Another polio victim was the African-American track star Wilma Rudolph. Shortly after birth she suffered from double pneumonia, scarlet fever, and polio. Her left leg was so crippled that doctors told her she would never walk correctly. But one day, after years of therapy and work, she threw off her leg braces and walked down the aisle of her church. In 1960, she became the fastest woman runner in the world, winning three gold medals at the Olympics. She did not let polio slow her down.

In the year 2006, no one in the United States contracts polio. Still, the disease has hung on into the twenty-first century in a few parts of the world, such as India and Nigeria. As long as polio exists anywhere, the possibility remains that it could gain strength again as a worldwide crippler of young people.

Not all diseases can be conquered, but it is possible to get rid of the virus that causes polio. That is why the World Health Organization, with help from organizations such as the March of Dimes, Rotary International, and UNICEF, targeted the disease for eradication everywhere. The key: to get every child in the world vaccinated.

If this effort succeeds, polio would be only the second major disease ever to be eliminated as a threat to humans. The first, smallpox, was defeated in 1977. Will polio be next?

© March of Dimes